Jataun,
Thank you for reading my book!

To Find You

CERECE RENNIE MURPHY

© 2016 Cerece Rennie Murphy
Copyright © 2016 by Cerece Rennie Murphy

All rights reserved.

No part of this book may be reproduced in any form or by any electronic or mechanical means, including information storage and retrieval systems, without written permission from the author, except for the use of brief quotations in a book review.

This book is a work of fiction. Names, characters, businesses, organizations, places, events and incidents either are the product of the author's imagination or are used fictitiously. Any resemblance to actual persons, living or dead, events, or locales is entirely coincidental.

Cover Art by Anna Dittman

Cover Design by Kea Taylor, Imagine Photography

Book formatting and Design by Write Dream Repeat Book Design, LLC

Paperback ISBN: 978-0-9856210-7-0
Hardcover ISBN: 978-0-9856210-8-7

Library of Congress Control Number:

WWW.LIONSKYPUBLISHING.COM

Dedication

To My Creator who teaches me daily what it means and what it costs to love and be loved.

Acknowledgements

To my family and friends who know me well and love me anyway. You are everything that makes life worth living.

To Stephanie, Quiana and Jessica, the most awesomest of editors (See, I know that drives you crazy!) Thank you for keeping me honest and making me look good.

To Tracy, Krystle, Ella and the many readers, bloggers and fans who spread the word about my work ~ thank you from the very bottom of my heart!

Part I

IN THE BEGINNING
1754, Gold Coast, Ghana

~

I WAIT FOR HIM here at the place where the night sky and the earth become lovers. In the tall grass of our homeland, between two kingdoms, we meet.

Getting here early is easier than slipping away late, especially now when life in my village is bustling with the preparations for our wedding in just three days.

But as the reeds lick the backs of my calves, I know that this is only one part of the reason I wait.

The truth is that I like to feel him coming. At this hour, when my imagination reigns over every shape and whisper, I can almost see him walking on limbs taller and stronger than mine will ever be. He cuts through the night that hides his slightly lighter shade and stalks his prey. I cannot hear his approach, but I feel him drawing near, compelled by the same force that holds me where I stand—the scent of my desire in the air.

I close my eyes and breathe deeply, imagining I can taste him, too. The flavor is salt, sweet grass, and home. It fills my senses and makes me thirsty.

On the outside, my knees shake and my heart pounds, impatient for its mate, while the deepest part of me grows calm and still—stretching towards the peace that only his presence brings.

And he's close now, so close.

When we were children, Ekow was such a scrawny thing. I used to like to wrestle him just to beat him, just to prove that I could. I was young, determined and more than a little jealous of the physical prowess of my older brothers. Secretly, I wanted to be like them, but my youngest brother, Kofi, was already 10 years my senior by the time I could walk. With Ekow, I knew I'd finally found a way to prove that no boy could match me.

My laughter rumbles in the stillness as I think of it. Oh, how angry he would be every time I beat him! And in the beginning, there were many, many times when I did. He would get so upset that his ears would twitch. He would stomp away from his defeat with his hands balled up in knobby little fists—eyes glaring, ears twitching, while one of our elders cackled nearby with me sticking out my tongue. We didn't see each other often enough for me to beat him every day, but I looked forward to it whenever I could. I was always stronger than I looked, and even when he grew a little taller than me, his limbs seemed to flail awkwardly about him so that he was never quite coordinated. And in my delicious reign as his tormentor, time seemed to stretch on forever, until one day, it stopped.

I remember the sun burned low in the sky that day as the dust and amber light conspired against me in swirling fits that stung my eyes. Rolling around on the ground, I was shocked to find myself panting for air. Suddenly, his legs overpowered me. I couldn't throw him the way I had been able to before. His grip was a vice that I had to sweat to free myself from, and even then, he could catch me again, quickly—too quickly for my liking.

Unable to break free, I grunted and cursed as he pinned me down on my back. At first, I refused to meet his gaze. Beneath my eyelashes, I could swear I saw my own taunting smirk, the same one I had given him year after year, curling the corners of his lips. Enraged, I shut my eyes and kicked my legs furiously, all to no avail. I could feel the muscles of his powerful thighs holding me in place without the slightest indication of strain, and I couldn't stand it.

As if sensing the scream that would send my brothers flying to my aid, he suddenly lifted his body from mine, then leaned over to adjust his grip so that our hands were stretched out above my head, palm to palm, fingers intertwined in the grass and the dirt beneath us.

How did I not know, even then . . . ?

Something about the gesture was so strange that it distracted me from my fury. The feel of his hands pressed firmly into mine made my stomach flutter and clench in a way that was startling, but not unpleasant.

"Ama," he called. "Ama, don't scream. Ama, please, surrender."

It must have been the "surrender" that made my eyes fly open to meet his in absolute indignation.

Sometimes I like to think that if I'd never opened my eyes, it never would have happened, but this is, of course, foolish. I was meant to see.

I looked up to find him staring down at me. The smirk I'd feared was nowhere in sight.

Instead, his eyes held the same wariness I felt as I looked back at him, then quickly dissolved into something I'd never seen in him before.

He eyed my mouth with what I understand now as a mixture of surprise and captivation. Back then, I still had no idea what was happening, but as his gaze lingered, I began to feel that someone was seeing me truly for the first time in my life. I remember fighting the nameless emotion that closed my throat and pricked my eyes.

"Ama, surrender," he whispered, "Please."

And that's when I understood that I held him in place as much as he held me.

"Please," he said again, and I finally realized what I needed to do all along.

Seeing the answer there in my eyes, he released my hands and rose to his feet. I remember averting my eyes against the sudden rush of loneliness that came as he left. But at the corner of my vision, I saw it, his hand extended out to help me up. He'd done it before, even as I beat him and he'd risen in defeat while I remained holding my belly in victorious laughter on the ground. I'd always ignored the gesture until that moment, when suddenly it felt like the most natural thing in the world to accept his help.

When I finally stood, I noticed for the first time that he'd grown at least 10 inches since the last time I saw him.

Despite my daze, I frowned. "You're taller than me," I said in dismay.

"No, Ama," he replied. Ekow's voice was deep, yet gentle as he stepped forward to take my other hand in his. "Now, we are exactly the same height."

I was 11 years old; Ekow was 13, and after that, nothing between us was ever the same.

With my eyes closed, it takes only a moment for him to close the distance. His hands cover my shoulders as his lips trace the curve of my neck. This is our greeting. No words. We speak in action.

I let my head fall back against his chest and feel his smile press into my skin at the place where my hum echoes deepest. He knows it is a sound I make only for him. When I turn to face him, I need no invitation. I wrap both hands around his neck and pull him closer, touching his lips to mine gently, feeling their full weight and softness. It is a chaste kiss, though I don't know why I do this. There is nothing chaste about why we are here. We are as ravenous as love itself, but I always feel the need to honor this power between us before we are consumed.

But one thing always leads to another, and as I pull him closer, lifting my chest to his, reverence gives way to something else entirely.

He lifts me in one quick motion onto him then lowers me down to the ground on his lap. We are a frenzy of arms and kisses, tongues tasting, teeth nibbling, and skin yearning to be closer still. His hands are in my hair, kneading my scalp as his kiss deepens. My mouth and my legs open wider in unison. Tears sting my eyes with every sensation I feel. I want to cry and laugh and scream. But the release is like the edge of a precipice I don't know how to jump off of, and so I choose to move instead, rocking against him slowly.

His eyes are open as he kisses me, watching my mood, reading my signs. Caressing my back his fingers move up and down my spine, loosening, unfastening, until I am naked in his lap. I look down in surprise to find that he is too.

My expression makes him chuckle with pride, knowing and devilish. And if it wasn't for the same power that I have over him, I would be terrified to be so taken with him. Because, in moments like this, the love I feel is so overwhelming that I'm sure the need to give it will break me in two.

How can I love one person this much and survive?

As Ekow lays our bodies down, I find myself sucked into the silence between death and creation. The fear slips between us like a foreign substance, threatening to cut the very fabric of which we are made, but Ekow will have none of it. With a heart that knows me, and steady, faithful hands, he reaches into the darkness and pulls me back.

Shaking his head, he takes my hand and kisses each finger before bringing them to his chest.

"It's just us, Ama. It's just us."

And I know it again, as always. My tears release the weight of silence as something new is born and an even deeper love takes its first breath. I watch him wait as the tide of my emotions recedes enough for me to breathe and expand.

I feel the lightness of it, and it makes me smile. From his questioning eyes, I know that he doesn't quite understand what's happened, but it only takes a moment for me to show him. I pull him into my kiss and pour everything that I know, everything that I am into it. Above me, he's breathless, enchanted by the ferocity of my caress.

I pull him closer still and feel the weight of him pressing at my opening. Large and insistent. Yet, he lingers.

It drives me crazy.

The muscles in my thighs twitch and tremble with desire. Vaguely, I recall that I'm not supposed to open so readily. Auntie says I should tease a man, make him beg for my sweetness, but I no longer care. There is no room for pretense between us and his eyes tell me it wouldn't matter anyway.

He knows what is his.

I squirm underneath him anxiously—half desperate, half greedy, and all in a rush, but he holds me still with the weight of his body as he slowly pushes inside.

And whatever feeling I had, whatever thought was racing, becomes silent. My whole being becomes focused on the path he is taking. I close my eyes and feel—wanting more, wanting everything all at once.

"Open your eyes. Look at me, Ama."

I struggle to find the focus to do what he asks, but then his hand comes up to rest on my forehead. I feel his thumb gently stroking my hairline as the heat from his touch settles into my skin. I open my eyes to find that he is cradling me from my head to the very tips of my toes, from the inside out he surrounds me.

I find his eyes and I can't help returning the wonder and joy that I see in them.

I will never be as safe as I am now. The realization makes the air itself burn in my throat as my tears begin to swell.

He holds us still as time hovers.

It is perfect, until I let out a shuddering breath that seems to weaken his resolve. He presses his forehead to mine and kisses me deeper, harder and then we start to move. And there is nothing and no one else who could reach me in this moment. I surrender to him as he surrenders to me—affirming that we are one being in the world that we create.

There is nothing quick or rushed in how he moves over me. It is not always like this when we come together, but tonight he savors every stroke and makes me do the same. Our legs twist and intertwine with the slim reeds of grass that bend into our makeshift bed and dance in the cool breeze around us. He keeps my head in his palm while seeking out my fingers with his other hand. With our palms pressed together, fingers intertwined, I fall deeper in love with every second that passes.

Though our marriage ceremony has yet to be, I know we have loved each other from the beginning of forever. The thought makes my hips rise in celebration. In response, he spreads me wider, presses deeper until I'm quivering, incoherent bliss.

His kisses flutter at the edge of my skin, but I feel them deep in my bones. He's whispering something to me that I sense more than hear. He is professing what I already know.

He loves me

As I love him.

I say the words back to him though there is no need. We witness to the Spirits, the air between us, and the beckoning light that tells us that it is time to part.

He holds me tight enough to feel it long after he's gone before disappearing into the brush. His quick feet are light against the ground as he runs, but I can still hear the sounds of his joy, hooting and howling at the dawn. There's no need to be quiet. He's already late for the morning fishing, and with the grin he'll surely be wearing when he gets there, it won't be hard for his brothers to guess why.

As I walk back to the place that will only be my home for a little longer, I'm sure that everything must be right with the world for him to be with me and me with him. So perfect. His presence lingers deliciously in the ache of my limbs and the smell of him on my skin. The thought makes me smile as I look forward to everything life together will bring. So lost was I in my daydreams, that I was completely unprepared for the sight of what was to come when I returned to my village.

But I should have known. If I were not so distracted, I would have caught the foul stench of burning flesh in the air.

Of the six Fanti tribes that surrounded my father, Chief Kodwo's, kingdom of Akumfi, there wasn't a single one that had not accepted, if not rejoiced, at our marriage. The union between Ekow and I was made barely a month after my birth, back when the seven kingdoms were more or less equal in wealth and numbers. But, as I grew, so did my father's wealth. His investments in the training of our goldsmiths had paid off with lucrative trades as far as the Orient and with it brought new people seeking to be a part of our prosperity. My father became known as a fair and just ruler, which increased his popularity among other chiefs and their people.

With our military numbers, there was never a challenge to our land, but my father was also careful to share our wealth and resources with the neighboring kingdoms in an effort to maintain peaceful relations. It was an effective plan, one that had diffused every threat and conflict the kingdom had encountered over the last 15 years. But while my father's strategy was sound against logical threats, it was defenseless against the simple, irrational emotion of jealousy.

Chief Kwesi of the Anyan kingdom and Chief Kobena of the Ejumako kingdom were long considered the least favorite of the seven chiefs. In addition to both having boastful and moody dispositions, they were also infamous for their less than honest trading habits. They cooperated with the other tribes because co-operation was necessary for all of us to survive, but they were never favored. Until recently, they didn't even seem to like each other.

Between them, the one claim they shared and fought over was the legendary beauty of their daughters. Throughout the Fanti kingdoms, their daughters were greatly sought after and this allowed the two chiefs to make strategic alliances through marriage. In fact, two of my eldest brothers had been married to a daughter from each kingdom.

But, despite the many wives between Chief Kobena and Chief Kwesi, they never had a single son, which left them out of the running when I was born and a marriage match needed to be made. The only male of suitable age and stature was the 2nd eldest son of the Nsukum kingdom, which was led by Chief Ato, a lifelong friend and confidante of my father. Since their son had been born on a Thursday, his mother named him Ekow. Our impending marriage, combined with the easy alliance between our fathers, soon made Nsukum the 2nd richest state in the kingdoms, much to the silent indignation of Chiefs Kwesi and Kobena.

As is Fanti tradition, though our betrothal was made at birth, the Visiting ceremony, which signifies the official start of our engagement did not take place until a few months before our wedding was scheduled to occur. So after the Visiting ceremony, when the wedding date was announced, all of the clans were surprised when Chief Kobena insisted on hosting a night of celebration in honor of our union.

By all accounts, the gathering for our wedding was unprecedented in the history of the Kingdoms. Never before had Chiefs and dignitaries from all seven states gathered for one wedding. Seven days of celebrations were to be had, in honor of the occasion and the long held peace between the Fanti nations, with each day being sponsored by a different kingdom.

Of course, everyone from Ekow's family and mine knew that these grandiose gestures had more to do with jostling for political power than any affirmation of unity, but, my mother insisted that it would have been rude to refuse their generosity, false though it was. So, we endured. The governing Asafo members agreed that, for the celebrations, the soldiers of each clan would stay outside the perimeter of our Kingdom, with only ceremonial guards allowed into the celebration, as a show of trust. We all should have been suspicious, but then again, nothing like this had ever happened before, and in my father's good heart, I knew he hoped that the celebration would deepen the bonds between the kingdoms.

On the 7th day before the wedding, the ceremonies began in the late morning and went on all day, which would have driven me insane except that with all my expected "preparations" for marriage, I was excused from attending most activities. This, of course, made it even easier for Ekow and me to slip away unnoticed. For 3 days and 3 nights, everyone in my village danced, ate and drank well past the burning out of midnight stars, until the morning of the 4th day, when the screams of my brother, Kofi, who was head of our military, broke through the borders of our village with a cry that was sounded too late.

When I stepped into the clearing of our village, I could see how it began. My brother, Kofi, lay before my father, twisted by the pain of death with the open wound of a spear tip through his shoulder and a machete buried deep in his back. With his gentle voice made hoarse from yelling, I could almost hear him calling from the tall grass that surrounded our home. Only after being bloodied from the battle would he have run from the perimeter, the lone survivor of a vicious attack he had not seen coming. He would have rushed to warn us, to save his hero and best friend. He would have run straight to our father. With haste he would have come, smelling the smoke and hearing the first of the screams. Blinded by love and fear, he would have stepped into the clearing and come upon the sight of our father with a spear driven deep into his chest, eyes open as he sat in a pool of his own blood. Kofi would have cried then, because of all of us who loved my father, Kofi loved him best. His grief, more than the pain of his injuries, would have brought him to his knees, allowing the assassin to take his chance as only a coward could, silent, in the back and cloaked in friendship. Kofi would never see who took his life, but I knew the markings on the machete were an emblem of the Ejumako clan.

Before recognizing the symbol, I was only vaguely aware of the chaos around me, but this new knowledge brought it sharply into focus. The neat homes and buildings that made up my village were all in flames, with piles of bodies lining the pathways. Even the sacred stools that symbolized the presence of our ancestors were splintered, discarded like refuse in the road.

The sound of panicked screams and wailing filled the air before they were muffled or simply snuffed out, one-by-one. But the singular pieces still failed to bring the whole of what was happening to my mind until I saw my mother's face staring back at me with cold, lifeless eyes.

She lay on the ground, darkened by shadow and ash just a few feet behind my father, which is why I had not seen her before. Most of her body was buried under rubble, save for her shoulders and arms, which were flung out and limp on the ground. Her severed head was only an inch from where the rest of her lay. In her hands she clutched a knife, too clean to have succeeded in completing whatever mission she had for it. But the blade called, almost as if in her dying moment my mother had seen that I would be standing just here and handed it to me.

Standing there, between the broken bodies of my mother, my father and my brother, I realized that I was most likely the only surviving member of my family. Rage and bitterness washed over me like a fever, just as I heard the traitor speak.

"Get her!"

I recognized the voice immediately and turned to it as three men came towards me, but I kept my focus on the one in the middle.

"My dear, Ama, I feared that somehow we had missed you, but I see you are just in time," Chief Kobena said with his usual smug grin.

My grandmother told me never to speak to the devil, lest he answer you back, so I did not respond. I had no idea how I would kill Chief Kobena. He was flanked by a guard on each side, but, somehow, I knew that I would.

I began to back away slowly, too slowly to evade capture, but that was not my aim. I only needed an advantage, a few seconds between us and a weapon. Though Kofi had been 10 years older, he'd always made time for me as a child. Behind our mother's back, he was the one who taught me how to wrestle and fight like a boy. "You're small, but you're strong," he used to say. "Use what you have to defeat your enemy." I could hear his voice as clearly as if he were whispering in my ear. Briefly, I looked down on the ground for anything I could use as a weapon and found my mother's dagger shining in the early morning light.

Kofi had also taught me how to throw a knife.

Reaching down quickly, I grabbed the dagger from my mother's hand, silently thanking her for giving me everything I ever needed, every second of my life. Though I'd never seen it before, I knew just by touch that it was the finest blade I'd ever held. Built for a warrior, but carved to fit inside a lady's hand. Certainly my mother had been both. I'll never forget how light it felt as I aimed and hurled it through the air. It didn't make a sound and nor did its victim, as the blade buried its sheath deep into Chief Kobena's skull.

The two men that reached the distance Chief Kobena would never cross grabbed my arms and threw me to the ground. The impact left a vacuum in my lungs that made me buckle and gasp. Curled onto my side, I clutched my chest, afraid that I would die until I saw death staring back at me.

Sheer will forced air back into my lungs so that I could scream. It seemed to me then, that everyone I knew, everyone I'd played with, and everyone I'd loved had been piled into burning mounds of flesh and bone. Some eyes were closed, others were frozen open in testament to the terror that stole their last breath, but they all pitied me and the terrible road I had just begun to travel.

After that, I remember the pressure, but none of the pain of my first experience with brutality. Somehow, I made it to my feet as they bound my hands and pushed me forward into a line of women and men I barely knew. But it didn't matter, none of us were who we had been even hours ago.

And that's when I thought of him. His family was not set to arrive until later on this afternoon. If what I believed about what had happened to us was true, had the treachery of Chief Kobena's plan escaped them? Would they hear about what happened in time to help those of us who survived, or had the same fate befallen them, too?

At first, I told myself that Ekow had escaped. That the destruction of my family had been payment enough for whatever wrong Chief Kobena believed had been committed and that the Nsukum kingdom would somehow be spared. But even as I played the story over in my mind, I sensed that hope was too precious a thing to carry on the road we were headed. Everything Ekow and I had wanted, everything our union was supposed to build, had been destroyed. I didn't think I had the courage to hope, but some things are too hard to deny and in between the lashes and the shouts, the moans and the cries that made up our long march east, I found myself wondering . . . *where is he?*

I don't remember much of the journey to the shore, though surely I was dragged here. The only thing that stayed with me was the gathering sound of the crows that followed us to our doom. By the time we reached our destination, my wrists and ankles were raw with blisters threatening to break. I had seen the ocean only once before when my brothers took me on a trading journey. Back then, the sight of the sea had filled me with wild curiosity, but now, all I felt was dread.

Everyone . . . everyone I knew was either dead or in chains. I envied my newly ascended elders and feared like never before for those of us whom death had not taken. Terror was everywhere I looked. There was no difference between the men and the women in this place; we were all helpless.

I'm sure I would have looked the same as them except for my unrelenting hope of finding him. And so I searched for Ekow, even as I dreaded finding him among the rest of the living dead. But the more I looked, the more I saw the magnitude of what was about to happen. Hundreds and hundreds of lives destroyed. The devastation was like poison in the air and the more I took in, I knew that there was no place among this horror that I would want him to be. And so I began to pray that he was not here.

We stood crowded together for hours in the mid-day sun, until I found something I did not expect, the missing piece to the puzzle of our betrayal. Even when I saw Chief Kobena in my village, I knew instinctively that no matter how conniving, Chief Kobena was neither smart nor powerful enough to plot or execute such an elaborate plan on his own.

As I watched a man I recognized from Chief Kwesi's personal guard arguing with a pale man in strange clothes, I knew he was the true mastermind behind the attack on my family. I watched with renewed anger as their arguing finally ceased and two small trunks were brought out and placed at the guard's feet. There were hundreds of prisoners in our group and it seemed ludicrous that our collective worth could be reduced to anything that would fit in so small a space. But it wasn't hard for me to guess the nature of their transaction. All of us had been sold to serve a master and begin a life from which we would never return.

I knew then that there was no hope of being saved. They were too many of us in chains and too many others left behind to season the earth with their blood. But my spirit was desperate for the comfort of him and so I looked around once more until my heart sank with relief and despair at not finding him.

And then somehow I heard it above the cries and chaos around us, a roar more vicious than any lion and the sound of chains being shaken in a battle of wills. Those who had already been broken shrunk from the commotion as if the very sight of a struggle shamed them into further resignation, leaving a blessed opening where I could see him through the crowd.

Even in chains, Ekow was magnificent, unequaled and untamed by his captors. It took two of them to hold him while the third got dragged from behind. I must've pulled the whole line of women I was chained with to the edge of the clearing just to be closer to him.

But, by then, he'd already seen me and by then, I'd wished he hadn't.

The sight of me and the evidence of all his unanswered prayers, identical to mine, took all the fight from his eyes.

It was in that moment I finally understood how truly hopeless our situation was. The fear and sadness in his eyes swallowed me whole, bringing tears to my eyes before I could stop them. Once he saw me, Ekow stopped moving and in doing so caught the men holding him off balance, so that in the sudden silence, the broken sound of my name on his lips reached over the crowd.

It was too late before I realized how I had unwittingly exposed our enemies to the only weakness Ekow had. The pale man in front, the one with filthy clothes, looked from me to Ekow for only a second, but it was enough. A spark of understanding flashed across his face and with a menacing grin, he dropped one end of Ekow's chains.

"I know how to keep this one in check," he said as he strode towards me quickly. After unlocking the chains from around my neck and legs, he yanked me from the crowd where I stood—too horrified to move.

"No! Do Not Touch Her!" Ekow roared. "You have no right!"

I understood the mistake immediately, though I was too afraid to turn and see the consequences in Ekow's eyes. Instead, I felt the man's grip on my arm tighten as he turned his gaze towards Ekow in cruel amusement.

"Oh, so you like this one, do ya? Well, so do I. If you keep giving us trouble, I'll take it *all* out on her. Ya understand me, darkie?" When he finished speaking, he pulled me close, pressing his body to mine as his eyes hovered salaciously over my shoulders and breasts.

We didn't understand his words, but we both knew exactly what he meant.

Ekow's face turned from naked emotion to unreadable in an instant. The expression was so unfamiliar to me that I almost didn't recognize him, but I understood. Our emotions were sacred things that belonged only to us. Ekow would not share his love for me with these beasts.

And it almost worked, except for the fury that made his ears twitch and his arms shake uncontrollably.

"Oh yes, she'll do nicely," the man said as he turned his rotten breath towards me and ran his hand down the side of my breast. My body shrank back instinctively. It had never occurred to me to hide the beauty of my own body before that moment. I closed my eyes against the sight and smell of him and because I did so, I didn't see what happened next. I only heard the screams.

In a burst of rage, Ekow's left arm broke free from the man who had expended all his might to hold him back. His fist swung out wildly, causing the man to his left to stumble back while hitting the man on his right squarely in the face. Blood gushed from his nose as he fell to the ground screaming.

With only one man to go, Ekow curled his body inward, using his right hand to seize the jaw of the man who gripped his left arm in vain. His shriek was piercing but brief as Ekow broke his neck in one swift movement. By the time I opened my eyes again, it was over.

"I'll kill you!" My beloved shouted at the man who still held me close, as three others rushed forward to take the place of those who had fallen.

"Shoot, him! Shoot him, NOW!" I heard someone shout, but I didn't understand until I saw the man beside me pull a strange metal object from a belt on his hip and point it at Ekow.

I did not know their language.

I did not know their names or customs, but I knew his actions meant death for the one person I could not bear to lose.

If we were to survive, if any of us were to survive, Ekow must live.

There was no thought in what I did next.

I reached for the man's hand and gripped the side of the metal object just as it erupted in flame. I could smell the burned flesh on my fingers, but I couldn't feel it as I screamed Ekow's name. Our eyes met in time for me to see one of the pale men standing closest to Ekow drop to the ground, convulsing as blood pulsed from a hole in his neck.

As the second man on Ekow's left went to help the dying man, Ekow wasted no time using the diversion to his advantage. With both arms free and only one man left to contain him, Ekow brought the elbow of his right arm down onto the collarbone of the last man standing. It looked easy because it was. They should have known better than to send someone of only average size and build to guard him. My Ekow was a warrior, made of over 6 feet of hardened muscle and bone. The man went down screaming.

More men rushed to the docks towards Ekow, but it was no use—the brace around his neck was now connected to three loose chains, one of which he held in each hand, whipping them mercilessly against anyone who was foolish enough to come near him.

I watched him in awe. Despite his bloodied feet, the loss of his home, our whole world, he was unbroken.

Nothing, I thought. *Nothing can stop him.* And though I couldn't see his face, I knew his purpose. With every lash of his chain, he drew a little closer to me. The proximity to the only thing I wanted in the world was dreamlike, and so I barely noticed when the retched man beside me suddenly pushed me away. For a moment, I was even grateful for the rush of fresh air.

"She ain't worth it." I heard him say as he aimed his metal weapon at me. I didn't know what he meant and I didn't care. I never took my eyes off of Ekow even when I heard the awful cracking sound again and felt what seemed like a burning spear rip through my chest.

The gasp I made was small, too small for anyone to hear, but him.

When Ekow turned towards me, the sound he made was wild—as furious and shapeless as the wind. It was nothing like my lion's roar. It was, I thought, the worst sound a man could make.

I watched him in a horrible waking dream as his mouth hung open, eyes full of tears. By the time I made out the sound of my name amongst his screams, I was already drifting away.

Though I felt the ground beneath me, my sight had expanded beyond. I could see my own body bleeding with a wound similar to the one made before by the strange metal weapon, the horror of the ship, the great stone fortress, and the water beyond as countless souls crowded the dock. I could see everything below me—my people in chains and the ruthless men who shackled and whipped them.

Everything in me was glad to leave the ugliness of this place, except for the screams that called my name. Except for Ekow. From far away, I could still see his face. Furious and broken, yet determined to live long enough to avenge my death, to free our people and find me again, in this life or the next.

And in that moment, I felt love breaking me open again, into the silence between life and death to create something entirely new, and though I had no desire to return to the terror of this earth,

I knew I would,

Again and again,

To find him.

Part II

STRANGERS
February 2, 1857 ~ Delhi, India

We keep the cheap liquor on the top shelf. The customers who ask for it pay more, but they deserve less. It was not always so. I changed it after my father died, before the war came in earnest and the first of these drunken imbeciles tried to take liberties with my mother.

It is not easy for a girl in my country to run a bar. In fact, I'm sure somewhere it is forbidden, but there is no one else, so it doesn't matter. I drained the last of my childhood crying over all the forbidden things that seem to happen anyway.

When the British first began taking our lands by right of their made-up rules, my uncles fought to defend our family's inheritance, while my father—the explorer, the constant traveler—stayed home to protect us. But their choices made no difference; none of them survived.

It's a good thing I have a boy's name—a testament to the wishful thinking and stubborn resolve of my parents. When I sign the deposit record and have my younger brother bring them into the bank, no one says a word. All the men are amazed at what a clever boy "little Satish" is to manage the family business so well at only 9 years old. For this reason, I'm convinced that most men must be very stupid, but I suppose this judgment is not entirely fair. Since the expansion of control by England's East India Company, our city is full of strangers who do not know us, and the few who linger from before understand why things need to be the way they are.

So, I keep the cheap stuff on the top of our mirrored, three-tiered display in the bar that was once the pride and joy of our community. The middle shelf carries the best we offer and is reserved for those who are least offensive. The bottom shelf, well, no one wants to be served from the bottom shelf, so I keep our talismans there, all the statues and gods that I pray to in hopes that my mother, my little brother, Nahil, and I will survive this place that used to be our home.

It helps that I'm ugly, too . . . or, at least, I used to be. In the year and a half since my father died, beauty seems more of a curse than anything else, forcing temptation, obligation and all manner of ill-intent on those it touches. When you're ugly, people don't pay you much attention. They expect less, so you get to do more.

My aunt used to say that I was so plain, despite my mother's elegance and beauty, because my father wanted an eldest boy so badly that the Gods made me look like one to please him. If my father ever agreed with her, he never let it show. He always told me that the Gods had been kind to him and that if I were too pretty too soon, my husband would come and snatch me away before he was ready to let me go. He used to tell me that he kept my beauty safe within his heart where only he could see it and that when the time was right, he would let it out. It was a silly notion, but one I cherished until the day he died.

I've often thought about my father's power to make things real just by saying them, because it was only after his death that people started noticing me. Mostly I get strange looks or a new awkwardness in my interactions with boys that annoys me, but I manage. I've been ugly longer than I've been pretty, and I don't have time to make whatever adjustments might be required. Suitable matches are hard to come by these days, but whenever my mother decides that one might present itself, my foul attitude usually makes the suitor's parents think twice, which is exactly how I want it. Survival, not marriage, is my only objective.

That is why I run the bar. It used to be a Chai khanas, a respectable teahouse for everyone in the neighborhood. At the end of the block, under a swaying canopy of blue glass lanterns and the heavy scent of spices from the market, our café, as father called it, was the toast of the town. In those days, mother would cook the most delicious treats and serve them on tiny silver trays that my father brought back from faraway places. We were also the only place for a hundred miles that had an accomplished pianist and a sitar player. People would come from nearby towns to hear my father play music from all over the world every night of the week. And as the candlelight twinkled off the mirrored walls, casting spells over us all, it was easy to give in to the feeling that we were worldly, wise and safe.

It was the café's reputation as a cosmopolitan place that brought the first of the British soldiers to our doorstep. My father died shortly after, no doubt from heartbreak over the utter corruption of his homeland by devils in linen suits. At the bar, they began to request liquor. They paid more, but respected us less. Still, we did what we had to do to survive. Now most of what we serve is liquor. My mother makes only the occasional samosa, trading in the best of her cooking for teacakes and other such tasteless food that the soldiers prefer.

The night I began tending bar started as any other, with my mother and brother out front taking orders and preparing drinks. Mahood and Guna were also there to help. The café was busy, but not overly so. Just enough work to justify the wages we paid for the extra help. I was in the kitchen cooking and washing dishes with my second cousin, Pashar, who would come to earn a little extra money from time-to-time. Halfway through the evening, while my mother was serving one of the British officers his drink, the man inquired on the whereabouts of my mother's husband. On hearing that my father was dead, he wasted no time offering my mother money for a look under her sari.

So far, no one has dared pay me the same disrespect, though I am younger and, at least theoretically, more desirable. I'd like to think it's the constant look of quiet loathing in my eyes that keeps them away, but if I am completely honest, I know I owe my reprieve to the stranger who sits at my bar almost every night since that night when my mother decided to confine herself to the kitchen.

When I think back to that moment, the events that transpired seemed to happen almost too quickly to have made such an impact. My mother's response to the officer's offense was uncharacteristically loud for a woman who is known for her quietness even more than her courtesy. From the kitchen I heard her scream, "How dare you! How dare you! I am a married woman!"

At the sound of her voice, I ran from the kitchen with the knife I'd been using to cut lemon wedges for tea. Without thinking I lashed out, slicing the hand that held the currency of his insult.

For a moment, I was hypnotized by the way the knife came back to me, half-coated with blood, and the happy sound of coins as they danced over the metal edge of the bar before spilling onto the floor.

Only then did I notice the wound I had inflicted as the officer grunted and cursed. The gash was deep and must have burned terribly with the juice from so many lemons embedded in his flesh. Over my mother's head, I could see my small statue of Shakti, the goddess of balance and destroyer of demonic forces, and I thanked her for the stroke of timing that had me cutting lemons so late at night.

When I looked up, the bloodied officer had already raised his other hand to strike. My only thought was to shield my mother. By then, I knew the type of danger I had exposed us to and was preparing for the worst.

It was almost 10 o'clock at night and the bar was more than half-full, with barely a familiar face among them. There was certainly no one who could help us, even if they wanted to. The jacket of the officer in front of me was full of medals, emblems and regalia. I was smart enough to know that meant he was someone of consequence, someone who could make life very difficult for us.

I did not expect what came next. I did not even see where he came from, this other officer, younger, taller, and strange, with pale hair and pale eyes like the fine ash that remains after a great fire has gone out. He looked at me for only a moment, then yanked the other officer's arm from where it hung, poised to strike in mid-air and brought it down on the edge of the bar hard. Mother gasped as we both heard the sharp snap of bone. I remember thinking that it was nothing more than he deserved.

Then, the older officer suddenly dropped out of sight. Somehow, the younger soldier had grabbed him by the shirt collar and thrown him out of our café and into the street.

"This is not a brothel!" the young soldier said in a growl that was deep and low. It was also final. The officer on the ground looked up at the younger soldier in terror. Clearly too afraid to even give voice to his pain, the man made no sound as three other soldiers quickly hoisted him up and carried him away.

My mother trembled in my arms, but my instincts told me that for tonight, at least, there would be nothing to fear. It had been almost two years since my father died and the first time since then that I'd felt safe.

But there was still no reason for me to trust this man, and as he walked back through the doors of our cafe, I cleaned off the knife and slipped it into my apron pocket, just in case my feelings of safety were wrong . He walked straight to the bar and looked directly at my mother and I.

"Please accept my sincerest apologies. I gave strict instructions that you were never to be disturbed." His voice trailed off as he looked away, his face betraying the same confusion I felt. I was certain I had never seen this man before.

"It doesn't matter," he continued. "There is no excuse. You have my word as an officer and a gentleman that it will not happen again."

"Thank you, officer . . . I'm sorry . . . I do not know your name," my mother said immediately, but I was still fighting my instincts. Why does he care how we're treated? How did he seem to know us when I had never seen him before?

"Forgive me. My name is August Mortimer, madam. Lieutenant August Mortimer."

"Well, thank you, Lt. Mortimer. My name is Mrs. Masir and this is my daughter, Satish."

I was still skeptical, but I nodded my head, so at least he would know that I appreciated what he'd done for us.

After the exchange, I guided my mother to the kitchen and assured her that I could and would manage the customers for the rest of the night. When she was settled, I returned to the bar to find Lt. Mortimer standing right where we'd left him, watching a clearly unsettling sight in the mirror.

When I followed his gaze, all I found was a man staring back at his own reflection, as if seeing it for the first time. Like so many habits of these foreigners, I thought it was odd, but dismissed it, prepared to leave him to his strange ritual. Then it occurred to me that part of the reason for his lingering presence might be that he was expecting compensation for his good deed. Mustering up the manners I was raised with, I approached him as politely as I could.

"I thank you again for your kindness, Lieutenant. Can I offer you a drink as payment for your assistance to my family?"

My voice seemed to startle him as he turned his haunted expression on me.

He was very tall. I knew that the moment I saw him, but when he turned from the mirror and looked at me, his presence felt suddenly overwhelming and I backed away.

"Thank you. Yes, please. I believe that would do me good. Whiskey, if it's not too much trouble. Any whiskey will do. And I'll pay you, of course. I mean, I have money. There is no need to repay me for before. I didn't do it for that."

And just like that, the commanding soldier who had rescued us was gone. In his place stood someone who seemed painfully shy and unsure of himself, maybe even slightly bewildered. I suddenly understood why I hadn't seen him before. I could imagine the person before me hiding easily in a corner, shrinking away from any kind of attention. As if sensing my assessment, he met my gaze in painfully awkward fits and starts, so I turned around and reached for the middle shelf. That was the first time I'd met and served First Lieutenant August Mortimer at my counter, but what I didn't know is that he would come back every night there after.

I don't usually get into conversations with men, partly because I don't often have the opportunity, but mostly because I don't like to waste time. From what I've observed, most men don't really care what women have to say anyway. At the bar, I see it all the time, men grinning and bearing their exchanges with women as they anxiously await their turn to talk or the moment when their patience will be rewarded with the affections they feel they've earned. Until recently, my father had been the only exception I'd seen.

This didn't bother me because I didn't want to talk with the men who came here anyway. I didn't want to have anything to do with them. If we'd had the money, we would have left this place a long time ago, but we didn't. And so, on occasion, I was forced to make conversation with men with whom I only wanted to keep my distance.

Which brings me to Lt. Mortimer who was a different sort of man altogether.

In the three weeks since he'd been coming to the bar (or that I'd noticed), I never saw him say more than a few words to any of the other soldiers who frequented the bar. In fact, it seemed to me that he held them at a distance and that the feeling was mutual.

But he went out of his way to talk with me, even when the effort seemed as difficult for him as it was for me.

It started simply enough. "How are you today?" and "Is your family originally from Delhi?" were questions I'd answered hundreds of times. Usually, once I asked what they wanted to order, the inexplicable need for chit-chat ceased, and there were no further attempts at pleasantry. I'd trained all of the regulars to do this. Most of them didn't even look at me anymore. They just grabbed a menu and ordered. It was just the way I wanted it. But Lt. Mortimer was either too slow or too determined for this type of training. After the usual questions were answered, he kept asking me things. He wanted to know where I had gone to school and how I'd learned to read. Even after I told him that both my parents could read and that they taught me how, he still wanted to know more.

It made me uncomfortable.

From what I'd seen and heard, it was dangerous to become friends with these foreigners. They were, after all, invading our country. Most seemed arrogant and superior in their dispositions, but Lt. Mortimer showed none of these failings.

Though his questions were relentless, his interest in my answers seemed genuine. He always remembered exactly where I left off in a conversation, and he leaned in closer than I cared for whenever my voice dropped too low for him to hear what I was saying. When we talked, his gaze on me was always steady and respectful, even though it rarely left me.

Also, Lt. Mortimer always did exactly what he said he would do. Whether it was remembering to bring a book or a photo, to arrive at a certain time or to leave when he was needed elsewhere. Everything he did was just as he'd promised. And his mouth was wide and full in a way that distracted me sometimes, but that last detail is hardly relevant since mostly what he did was annoy me.

One night, he even inquired about my statues.

"What are those things you keep on the bottom shelf there?" he'd asked. Lt. Mortimer had walked into the bar late that afternoon more morose than usual, but after several rounds of whiskey and staring into the glass mirror, he finally seemed to relax. I'd noticed him studying my figurines for most of the evening, but by the time he asked me about them, his speech was slightly slurred. I shrugged, not prepared to get into a discussion about my beliefs.

"You have your gods; we have ours," I answered.

"I don't believe in God," Lt. Mortimer declared before draining his finger of whiskey and placing it firmly down on the bar. The grin he gave me afterwards was wicked and unjustly proud. I'd never seen him look like that before, like a child daring me to play a game that would surely get us both in trouble.

I remember shaking my head and trying hard not to let the curve of his mouth affect me.

"I don't believe you," I answered back.

August leaned in then, suddenly taking this discussion very seriously. When he answered me, his speech was slower than usual as if trying to make sure he did not slur his words.

"No, madam. Do not mistake my drunkenness for insincerity. I swear it to be true."

His breath washed over me, warm and sweet, like the whiskey. I turned from him immediately.

"Where is my clean cloth?" I mumbled, focusing all my attention on the mindless task. I'm not ashamed to admit that I took all the time I could reasonably waste before pulling the cloth out from between two crates of dirty dishes. And in that time he had not moved an inch. He was still too close. Feeling a little on edge, I kept my eyes down and began wiping the counter.

He watched me until I was convinced that he enjoyed watching me squirm. The thought irritated me enough to gather my courage.

"If it were true, you wouldn't enjoy it so much," I admitted finally.

This made him laugh. The sound was intimate, open. It carried, but only a little. From the corner of my eyes, I saw him move even closer.

"Enjoy what? The disbelief?" he asked while turning his empty glass around in his hand. His fingers were long and nimble as the light reflected and refracted on the crystal, casting clipped rainbows everywhere. I watched, fascinated, until he caught me staring and met my eyes through long, dark lashes. There was something so familiar in the expression that it took my breath away. All of a sudden, I felt emboldened, exhilarated, and calmed all at the same time, for no good reason. I also realized that he was playing with me and enjoying it. If he insisted on trying to draw me out, then he should be willing to face the consequences. Two could play this game.

With my heart racing and a strange prickling sensation in my skin, I left the rag on the counter and turned to retrieve the bottle of good whiskey. I met his eyes where I knew I would find them, watching me in the mirror. But this time, I almost returned his smile.

"The rebellion, Lt. Mortimer," I said, speaking to his mirror image. By the time I turned around, I was pleased to note that he was still staring at his own reflection.

Reaching for his glass, I continued, "You wouldn't enjoy the rebellion half as much if you weren't sure you were offending some . . . greater authority."

The stunned expression on his face was priceless. I almost laughed out loud—almost. I slipped the glass from his fingers and began pouring without him seeming to notice. I stopped just before the rich brown liquid reached the rim.

By the time I handed him the glass, he looked absolutely perplexed. I was ecstatic to have finally gained the upper hand on this overly inquisitive man! Maybe now he would finally leave me in peace.

"I hope I haven't offended you, Lieutenant," I said sweetly.

He hesitated for a moment before replying in a sober tone, "No, not at all. I just . . . you are very observant. I hadn't quite thought of it that way before. You've challenged my thinking on the matter, which I suppose I wasn't expecting."

I excused myself then, proud of my small victory and fairly sure that he would find himself some other place to sit if he ever visited the bar again.

Later that night, while retelling the story to my mother, she looked at me strangely and warned me to be careful of becoming too fond of Lt. Mortimer. I remember rolling my eyes and laughing as I assured her that my antics had surely gotten rid of our best customer.

Of course, I was wrong.

Two days later he asked me why I was given a boy's name, and if he'd gotten the Hindu translation of it right. I'd never told him any of this, but somehow he'd found out on his own. At first, I was thrilled that he'd been curious enough about me to discover it, but then the understanding of the reason behind my own delight set in. How had I come to the place of wanting him to know me? When had that begun to mean so much? I couldn't afford to even speculate about the answers, not with him looking at me, not while he was standing so close.

Obviously I had to put a stop to this.

"Why are you doing this?" I asked.

"I beg your pardon? I don't understand what you mean." He leaned in again and smiled that particularly expectant smile that made his lips look even more distracting.

I backed up until my head hit the middle shelf.

"Careful there," he said in a voice full of concern.

"Why do you want to know what my name means? Why are you talking to me?" I hoped I sounded more annoyed than afraid.

He finally sat back on his barstool.

"I'm just trying to be polite. To . . . make conversation," he stammered.

"Well, that isn't necessary." I replied. "This is a bar. You drink. I serve. That's really all that is required."

He was smiling again, but it wasn't his expectant smile this time. It was sad and distant, and it made me feel unexpectedly cruel to have been the one to put it there.

"It must be true then, the translation of your name. My teacher told me that it means 'one who speaks truth.' I can see that you earn it. That is an uncommon trait in a woman, at least where

I'm from. I don't mean to bother you. I can sit somewhere else or leave, if you wish."

I averted my eyes. Regret was something that I rarely felt. My life was filled with things I had to do to survive, whether I liked them or not. In that context, remorse seemed like a waste of time to me. But this man had shown me nothing but decency, nothing but kindness. Regardless of our circumstances, that was worth something and I knew it. I found myself almost too ashamed to meet his gaze.

"I'm sorry I spoke so harshly. You have always—" For the first time, he cut me off before I could finish.

"There is no need for you to apologize," he began. "You have every reason to be suspicious of my motives. I understand completely."

Surprised, I looked up to find that he was still watching me with the same sad smile on his face. He looked hurt, but he made no effort to hide it from me, so I said the first thing that came to mind.

"Why are you learning Hindi?"

"Because . . ." he paused for a moment, weighing his words before leaning in again and holding me with a gaze from which I could not turn. "I'm trying to learn Hindi because I want to talk with you in the language you use with your family. Because I want to be someone you can trust even though there is no good reason why you should."

Though I knew it was rude, my mouth fell open. Inside I was at war with my instincts. No one besides my parents had ever taken this much interest in me. Somewhere inside I knew I could trust August, that in fact, I already did, but my head denied it, fought against the notion until my stomach felt queasy. But more than any of this, my mind kept posing a question that I could not answer.

Who is this man?

I don't know how long I stood there staring at him. Everything about him was wrong. Everything except for something else that I felt, but couldn't see, something else that seemed to matter more than all the rest.

"Satish, do you want me to leave? Tell me, truly, and I will never bother you again."

The very meaning of his words hurt, though at the time, I refused to acknowledge it. Why should I care if he leaves? But the truth, even if I only ever admitted it to myself, was that I did care.

I didn't know it was midnight until the clock chimed above my head, an absurd little thing called a cuckoo clock that my father had brought back from his travels. The sound made me jump while the man in front of me sat stock still.

My mother came out suddenly, as she always did at the close of the day, to take the money to the kitchen to be counted while I cleaned the tables. But the tense silence between Lt. Mortimer and myself must have stopped her in her tracks.

"Do you need anything else before we close, Officer?" my mother asked nervously as she looked from her customer to me.

"No, madam. I believe it is time for me to go," he replied. Though he answered my mother, his eyes lingered on me before turning to her at the last moment. "I know you have a lot of work ahead of you, Mrs. Masir, so I bid you good night," he said with a bow, then turned away.

I watched him as he announced to his men that it was time to go. And as always, like magic, men in varying stages of inebriation filed out of our little café in a single row with no quarrelling, no shoving and no mess. It never occurred to me until that moment why he was doing it, why he'd done it every night for the past 4 weeks. He was trying, in his own way, to be considerate, to help us.

I was stunned at all the things I had missed and the things I would miss if I let him walk away.

He was almost out the door before I found my ability to speak, but when I did, I made sure he could hear me.

"Lt. Mortimer! I would be honored to help you with your Hindi lessons . . . if you would like."

At the sound of his name he'd turned around, and by the time I finished saying what little I had the courage to say, the smile on his face held something I had not witnessed before in the short time I'd known him. For a brief moment, he looked happy.

"Tomorrow, then, madam. I will see you tomorrow."

And for the first time, I returned his smile. When he came back the next day, I started calling him August.

It took months for August to say even a sentence to me in Hindi, though he claimed he took lessons three times a week. But on the rare occasion when I could get him drunk, I got to hear phrases, words, or fragments of his thoughts in my language that would either make me giggle or make me blush, depending on what he chose to say.

We talked every night as often as we could but never for as long as we liked. The best talks were always late at night. After everyone left, August would stay and help me clean the tables. At first my mother would subtly object, nervous about his intentions, until slowly but surely he wore her down in the same way that he'd done with me, with kindness, respect, and patience.

While the bar was open, he was always cordial. As soon as he took his seat, the officer he walked in as would change into my friend. With growing ease he'd converse with me but always with a hint of the decorum fitting his rank and station. His back was always straight (unless I mumbled and he leaned in), his body always on alert. But after midnight, after the doors were locked and the curtains drawn, he would change again into just a person, a young man not much older than myself. His laugh was louder and his body fully relaxed. He tugged on his ear often and his expressions were so animated they were comical. I came to love the look of him in those twilight hours, the way he shed his exterior and became himself only for me.

Mostly we talked about our families—how odd and indispensable they were. I learned he had several brothers and sisters, but he was only close to one of them, a younger sister named Annalise whom he thought would have liked me very much. Then he learned why and exactly how much I hated each and every one of my father's seven sisters and how I thought they hated me back equally.

August told me about his grandmother, who he said played more of a role in raising him than even his parents. And I, in return, told him about my father, about how he loved us and what a magical place the world would become whenever he was around.

Sometimes we sat on the floor; sometimes we sat on the bar stools and shared food on the counter. Sometimes we would just stare at each other without saying much of anything at all. Those were the times that I knew I loved him most, in the midnight hours when everything is at once forbidden and possible.

We touched very little during those times: a stroke of my cheek, a shy squeeze of his hand, a brush of our shoulders together when we sat side by side. Every whisper felt intimate, sacred. Sometimes, I felt naked with how deeply he saw me, into me, as if no part of me was unacceptable to him. The things I hoped he'd noticed and the things I'd tried so hard to hide, he saw them. From my slight lisp to the roughness of my hands, he saw all my imperfections, smiled gently, and loved me still. And I tried my very best to see and understand him, too.

The only thing we never talked much about was his work with the East India Company, or "The Company," as everyone called it. At the start of our late night sessions, I asked what had brought him to India. "Foolhardiness," he replied with a bitter laugh and quickly changed the subject. He told me later that his father had been a highly decorated officer in the British military and that his family legacy in the military, combined with the exotic stories of India that he'd heard from his father's colleagues, enticed him to what he thought would be an adventure.

"And perhaps it was an adventure, in the beginning, but now it's something else, something I don't know if I want to be a part of anymore." Though I wanted to know more, I didn't press him. I already knew that he was not close to anyone he worked with and that his job didn't make him happy. Whatever story he needed to tell me, I knew that life would push it forward, and eventually it did.

I remember the night well because it was one of those rare occasions when August was not at the bar by 6pm. By the time he arrived, we were all busy serving a boisterous Friday night crowd. With a full house, I didn't have much time to speak with him, but when he came in, I immediately noticed that his normally pristine attire was slightly disheveled and that his right hand was red and slightly swollen. In between orders, I snuck him a small pouch filled with ice and a double shot of whiskey.

"Are you alright?" I asked, pushing the ice pack and the drink towards him.

"I just needed to see you, to hear your voice," was his only reply. I had no time to find out what he meant, but his sweet words did nothing to comfort me. In between serving customers, I watched him staring at himself with that familiar haunted expression. I hadn't seen it in a while, and the fact that it had returned alarmed me. In desperation, I went into the kitchen to ask Pashar to come out and help us so that I could get a moment to talk with him, but by the time I came back into the café, he was gone. Since we were first introduced, August had never left without saying goodbye.

The next day was Saturday and he didn't come. My stomach felt sick as the day dragged on. I realized then that I had no way of reaching him. I didn't know where he worked, where he lived or even if he had a friend with whom I could leave a message. We had talked so much, shared so much, but in the end, our worlds were completely separate, and it frightened me.

I should have known that he would come after midnight when the lines between our lives faded away. Mother had gone to bed, while I stayed downstairs to mop the dining room floors. I had just finished when I saw his shadow darken our doorway.

August stood there in a wrinkled linen shirt and pants as I unlocked the door to let him in.

"May I . . . is it alright? I just need to see you. I'm sorry I didn't come today. I thought I could change things, but I can't." It was the first thing he said to me, and though I could smell the liquor on his breath, I was sure he was sober. Whatever he'd drank didn't have the effect he'd planned.

"Of course, August," I replied, pulling him inside.

"I can help you clean up. I know it must have been busy today."

I gave him a look as if to ask how he knew, but then he leaned closer to cup my cheek within his hand.

"I've been here every day for three months, Satish. I know what your Saturday crowd looks like. I could probably name every person who was here."

I smiled, just glad to see his face and hear his voice. The warmth of his hand was comforting and everything I'd been missing all day.

"Can you serve drinks? Maybe I should hire you."

For this I got a tired little smile.

"Maybe," he whispered.

"Sit down, August, and tell me what's happened. You look like you haven't slept."

I led him to one of the soft cushioned booths at the far side of the room intending for us to sit down more comfortably, but instead he collapsed, stretching his whole body along the length of the booth with one arm covering his eyes.

I took the seat across from him with the small mahogany table between us lit only by the moon.

"I haven't slept, not yet," he admitted.

"Tell me, August."

"I failed them, Satish. I failed them."

"Who? What do you mean?"

"My men. Yesterday, two of my men were beaten, nearly to death, by other officers. I didn't know. I couldn't stop it."

"These are Indian soldiers, sepoys, under your command?"

"Yes, but the officers that beat them waited until I was off base. They knew I wouldn't allow it otherwise. They waited until I wasn't there, Satish. They disobeyed my direct orders so that they could prove a point. Now my soldiers know I can't protect them. I can't stop what's happening."

I tried my best to put the pieces together. I wanted to understand, to catch up to where he was, but I couldn't. There was too much about his world that I didn't know.

"What's happening, August? Why did they do this? I don't understand."

"It's the cartridges, the gunpowder cartridges. The Company sent new ones, ones that were supposed to be easier to load, but they were greased with animal fat. Pig, cow . . ."

I gasped. What I knew of guns and cartridges was very little, but I did know that the gun cartridges had to be bitten off to load the powder. I also knew that if they were covered in pig or cow fat, no Muslim or Hindu would defile themselves in such a way.

"How could they be so stupid?" I said in disgust. "How could they expect any sepoy to load a gun made in such a way?"

"I know. I know. At first we didn't know, but as soon as I found out, I removed the new cartridges from my regiment and ordered cartridges that were not greased, like the ones we'd used before. I told my commanding officers that neither my men nor I would be using the new cartridges. They resisted, but it's my regiment, so it's supposed to be my decision, but my commanding officers didn't like the way my orders made the other regiments look, so they went behind my back to prove a point."

"So they tried to force your men to use the cartridges . . ."

"And they refused . . ."

"And were beaten . . ."

"Yes."

"August, I . . . I don't understand. The sepoys work for The Company. The sepoys are their soldiers. Don't they have any respect for our religions, our culture?" My voice trailed off. What more could I say?

"Not anymore."

We sat in silence for a long time listening to the sound of an early summer rain that had just begun to fall.

"What will you do?" I asked finally.

"I don't know. If I leave, then there won't be any protection for the men who have followed me, and if I stay, I think they will consider it a betrayal, my acceptance of everything I've been trying to fight against."

August was right, of course, and we both knew it. After a few fruitless minutes of trying to come up with another solution, I let out a long sigh.

"Well, I think it's bad, either way," I said finally. "I can't offer a solution to your problem, but I can offer you some food. Would you like something to eat?"

August looked up at me and nodded. "Yes, thank you. I'm starving."

"Me, too," I said earnestly. "I was so worried about you that I didn't eat all day."

I'd intended for August to wait for me in the café, but he followed me into the kitchen, helping me warm up what food we had left. Sitting on the small cutting table in the kitchen, we ate everything in sight, and as we ate, he began to smile. So did I.

"This is wonderful. Thank you."

"What? You like eating in a tiny, dark kitchen?"

"I like eating with you."

I stuffed my face to keep my smile at bay, but I could feel him watching me. I kept my eyes on my plate until I heard him put his fork down.

Feigning outrage, I looked up. "It's rude to stare at people while they eat, you know. Surely they teach you that much in British schools!"

He ignored me and leaned in. "You're beautiful," he said softly.

For a moment, I froze, absorbing his words as they washed over me. No one but my parents had ever called me anything close to beautiful. No one had, up until that moment, and even if they did, I don't know that I would have believed them. But I believed August. With all my heart, I believed him, but that didn't make me ready to hear it.

I didn't realize my eyes were closed until he spoke.

"Satish, look at me."

The food in my mouth, which was at least twice the size of any normal bite a person should take, stuck in my throat like a stone. I tried to swallow, but none of my reflexes seemed to be working. I grabbed the water and filled my mouth, forcing everything down in one big gulp.

He waited patiently, as always, until I put down my glass and gathered my courage.

When I met his eyes, they were beaming. How could I be afraid of this?

"You are beautiful," he said again.

"Thank you," I replied. "So are you."

He laughed a little, reflecting my own awkwardness as we both looked down to see our fingers almost touching on the table. Slowly, his fingertips began to trace mine.

"What if . . ." His voice trailed off as his fingers interlaced with mine, first one hand, then the other.

He looked up at me again, our eyes meeting over the mingling of hands and fingers. I saw the yearning, the desire for all the things we had yet to share, all the things that we wanted that were too fragile to touch and too far to reach.

"What if . . ." I whispered back, just as I heard my mother's footsteps coming down the stairs. We waited until the very last moment to pull our hands apart.

Mother looked upset, but not surprised to find us together.

Before I showed him out, under my mother's watchful eye, I asked him, "So, what are you going to do about your men?"

"Keep fighting. Keep trying to make it right until I can't anymore."

"That sounds like a good plan," I said, hoping that he could hear the pride in my voice.

"I know," he whispered back. "I keep good counsel."

It was a quarter past four on a Sunday afternoon and August still had not come. The bar was busy with the usual mix of church-goers and heathens, although by this hour, it was hard to tell them apart. With the heat rippling off the ground since morning, our ceiling fans spun around uselessly in search of a breeze that never came. All around me the fine pressed linens of the sanctified sagged with perspiration as they blended in with the bed-rumpled clothes of men who woke up too late from last night's sins to seek absolution.

I busied myself amongst them, refilling goblets and tumblers with enough beer and liquor to dissolve whatever piety or regret lay between them. So that all our patrons were once again among equals, except, of course, for us.

August never went to church and was usually here early so that if I waited just a little, we could sit out back, eat breakfast, and talk a while before the crowd came. It was something that I looked forward to more then I cared to admit in recent weeks and this morning even more than others.

What if . . .

My mother had looked at me with foreboding when I went to bed last night. We stared at each other silently with my brother sleeping between us until I fell asleep. In her eyes, I felt the warning she would not say as loudly as if she'd screamed it in my ear, but I knew and she knew it was far too late.

Nothing was more real then the way his eyes traced every curve of my face. The way he leaned in whenever I spoke. I loved him as he loved me in some far off place where that was even possible yet somehow we made real with every touch of our hands. It was an impossible thing, and yet, it happened. It was happening.

I rose early that morning, waiting for him as my mother prepared our breakfast. She noticed that I saw her put two plates and a bit more aside, covering it carefully so that it would not spoil until he arrived. My smile of thanks was met with eyes that were pinched with worry as she ran her fingers through the hair I'd spent most of the morning brushing to a sheen.

"Once the morning crowd is settled, I will take Nahil and go to the market. We need supplies. I'll leave Mahood and Guna here with you. Do you think you can manage until my return?"

As my brother hooted and hollered his excitement around us, I nodded dumbly. Over the last few months, my mother had grown wary of leaving the bar, even to shop for necessities. In fact, she hadn't left the bar in weeks. That she would want to now, for a day-long trip, left me stunned.

"I thought you were afraid?" I asked in confusion.

"There is no safe place, Satish. Not anymore," my mother replied, then turned from me to unwrap the dough for the day's bread. Her words felt like a slap in the face, though whether or not she meant them to I had no way of knowing, so I asked her.

"If you didn't approve, Maji, why didn't you stop us?" My mother let out a long sigh before taking the first ball of dough into her hands.

"Because I have not forgotten what love looks like," she replied softly. "It was the same way with your father and I. His family did not want us to marry. They felt that he could have done better than me, but he would not hear of it. So, we left everything behind. That is how we came to live here, so far away from our family."

She looked up at me then with love and determination in her eyes. "They chose to lose their son rather than accept his choice. I would never make that mistake. I would never risk losing you, Satish, even if it means having a British officer for a son-in-law."

"Thank you, Maji. Thank you," was all I could say as I closed the distance between us and held her tightly.

"Go," she ordered, swiping at her eyes. "He will be here soon, I'm sure." Unable to control my smile, I tied the apron around my blue sari, the one August seemed to like best, and went from the kitchen to open the door in anticipation of our first customer.

But he didn't come early. He didn't come at all, and as the hours ticked on, I began to wonder if he regretted all the sweet things he'd said the night before. For the most part, I'd returned his overtures with silence while every emotion I felt burned in my throat, crowding out my words. But today was different. Today I'd planned to say it all.

When he didn't come by noon, doubt rushed in like water, drowning me in the silent space where I'd been trying not to think of the time. By one o'clock, I was convinced that everything had been a mistake: our talks, my trust, his very presence. By three, I was fighting back tears, a mirror image of all the silly girls I despised who cried into their saris over boys.

At 3:42pm he came, wild and sweaty, but his eyes went straight to me, and as they met, I knew that the reason he was late had nothing to do with us. Relief poured out of me in an unrestrained smile, beckoning him, but August hesitated at the door. His eyes darted around the room, counting all the people who spanned the distance between him and me. When he was finished, he looked up in desperation.

"हमें बात करने की जरूरत है" *We need to talk*, he mouthed in Hindi. My heart fluttered, excited by the notion that he would use my native tongue as our own secret language. In the kitchen, Pashar would be almost finished with the dishes from brunch as we prepared for the transition to the dinner menu. We could steal a moment there. I had just refilled each glass that was not already to the brim and even the most inebriated of our late-afternoon brood could surely wait five minutes.

I nodded quickly and motioned to the kitchen.

Waiting on the back porch, I half-expected a kiss when he came through the swinging doors moments later, but that is not quite what I got. After taking one look back into the kitchen, he grabbed my hand and pulled me further into the yard, until we were hidden from sight by the bed linens hanging on our clothesline.

"Where are your mother and brother?" he asked as he pulled me into our first true embrace. I couldn't see his face, but I could hear his heart pounding against the brass buttons of his uniform. The fear I heard there made me tighten my grip around his waist as I looked up into his eyes.

"They went to the market."

"When?"

"Just after one o'clock. August, what's wrong? You came so late today. I was worried," I began, but the look on his face silenced me. I had no idea what was going on, but I knew that this was not a time for fuss and idle chatter. So I waited and watched as his eyes traced the planes of my face, as they always did, until he was ready to answer me.

"Something terrible has happened. A war is coming," he whispered.

"What do you mean?" I tried to pull away, as if distance would make me understand his words more clearly, but he would not let me go.

"A mutiny. Some of the sepoy soldiers rebelled today in Meerut. They attacked officers, Satish, British officers, and killed them. We just received a telegraph that said the sepoy rebels are headed here—to Delhi."

"Now?"

"Yes, right now. They should be here by morning."

I wanted to ask why, but it would have been a stupid question. I knew why; we both did. You can do whatever you want, but never for as long as you want. It was always only a matter of time.

"They say the Muslim and the Hindu soldiers are working together," he mused as if surprised.

"We are all Indians," I said.

He looked at me as if the notion was new to him, then nodded. "You're right, of course. And this is your land. You have every right to defend it."

"What will happen if they reach Delhi? Is this about the cartridges? Aren't you trying to change that? Can't you make them stop using them?"

"I tried again today, Satish, but they refused to listen. I specifically requested cartridges that were not greased with animal fat, but they will take time to get here. Time we no longer have. Besides," he added while wiping away the sweat from the edges of my hair, "after Meerut, everything has changed. We . . . the British, will not stand for any dissension within the ranks. The Company will answer this threat with full force; there's too much at stake if they don't."

"But you can speak to the sepoy, explain to them what you're trying to do . . ."

I trailed off as August tilted his head and smiled that pitiful smile at me.

"Why would they trust me, Satish? I can't protect them and they know it. I couldn't stop two of my own soldiers from almost being beaten to death with their own guns for refusing to use the cartridges. Even though I tried, even though I punished the officers who disobeyed my orders, it didn't matter. I'm on the wrong side, Satish."

I knew he was right, even as I shook my head to deny it. I just couldn't accept that everything I'd hoped for was gone before it had even begun.

"If that's true, if there is nothing to be done but wait until this catches fire, then why did you come?" I blurted out angrily.

"Because I love you, Satish."

The words brought tears of joy and sorrow to my eyes all mixed together.

"I know I'm the wrong man from the wrong place; I've felt it my whole life. No matter where I was, I was always wrong somehow. I never belonged. Sometimes, I don't even recognize my own reflection—almost like I keep expecting to see someone or be someone that I'm not. It doesn't make any sense. Nothing made any sense before you. You are the only thing that has ever been right about me."

The familiar pressure of too much emotion weighed heavily again in my throat, constricting everything I wanted to say, but this time, I would not let it stop me.

"Then stay with me," I whispered. "Stay with me."

His fingertips were gentle as they moved up the side of my face and into my hair. August kept his eyes open, searching mine for permission and any sign of resistance as he grew closer.

I clutched onto the sleeves of his jacket, trying to accelerate his pace, but he took his time, until the bridge of his nose stroked mine, and I could taste the coolness of his breath on my tongue.

"I just . . ." he murmured before his eyes finally closed, and I reached up to the tips of my toes to close the distance between us.

I gasped as our lips touched, moving in unison with soft, slow kisses that pressed together like hands in prayer. His palms covered my cheeks as he drew me closer so that my whole body felt encased by him, glowing with warmth and light.

I didn't notice I was trembling until we'd stopped to breathe. Placing his forehead against mine, he kept his hands in my hair, massaging my scalp in a way that I could feel all the way down to the base of my spine.

"Stay with me," I whispered urgently, looking up into his face.

"Always," he whispered, then kissed me again.

※

By the time we went back inside, it was clear that the news of the sepoy revolt had spread. Half the room was empty, with bills and coins thrown haphazardly about in a clear rush to leave the premises. Those who remained talked in hush tones at the corners of the room while looking at our staff and me with new suspicion.

August was pensive as he took his usual spot at the bar and picked at the food I brought him. It was already a quarter to six and my mother and Nahil had not returned. She should have been home almost an hour ago. August insisted on waiting with me, then going to the market to look for them if they did not return by six, which is why he was still at our café when one of his petty officers stormed through the door looking for him.

"Sir," he began, brushing past me on his way to August, "General Flood requests your immediate presence at the base."

August took a long drink of water before looking up from his plate, but even then he did not turn to face the officer. Instead he stared straight ahead at his reflection in the mirror with the same expression he had the night we met.

But it didn't take long for the look of bewilderment that I remembered to dissolve into something hard and resolute.

"I'm not going anywhere," August said to his reflection. "This is where I belong."

"I'm sorry, Lt. Mortimer, but I'm under strict orders to bring you back, by force, if necessary. I was told—"

August smiled into the mirror.

"Do you think you could, Wesley? Bring me back by force?"

"August . . . I . . . Please, don't make me do this."

Slowly, August turned to face him. "Then don't make me. Leave here, Wesley, and don't come back."

Wesley's eyes widened in disbelief as he stared at the man who had once been his commanding officer.

"General Flood said you might resist, but I didn't believe him. You can't just abandon us, August! We're under attack. The sepoys will be here by morning. You know that! We need you to help keep our sepoys in line or we might have mutiny on our hands here, too!"

"Might?" August laughed bitterly. "Are you blind? It's already happening! Two of our best officers, Rafi and Sumeet, plus three soldiers under their command have already disappeared. By morning, half their regiment will be gone."

"How . . . how do you know this?" Wesley stammered.

August shook his head in disgust. "Because they were my men, and I was their commanding officer. I was responsible for them until General Flood overruled my orders. They left early this morning thanks to the flogging two of the soldiers under their command received for refusing to defy their own religion. They were nearly beaten to death, Wesley! When did we become these people?"

Wesley's back straightened. A chill ran through me as I watched contempt replace the concern in his eyes.

"We have always been these people, August. We are conquerors and you are one of us."

The truth of it hurt. I could see it in August's eyes, but he did not waiver. "Not anymore," he replied. "Not anymore."

"Did you have anything to do with their escape, August? Tell me the truth."

"They didn't escape, Wesley. They're not our slaves. They're free men in their own country, but no, I wasn't clever enough to have planted that idea in their heads, and it's obvious now that they didn't need me to, did they?"

I couldn't tell if Wesley believed August or not, but either way, it didn't matter.

"So you're abandoning us, then? And for what?" Wesley asked bitterly. He looked around the room, as if searching for the words, until his eyes settled upon me. "This . . . girl?"

August stood up quickly with his jaw set. He'd taken off his jacket a while ago, and from the strain in his bare forearms, I could tell that his fists were clenched. Immediately, Wesley backed away.

"Leave. Now," August commanded.

Wesley stumbled over chairs and tables as he backed his way out of the room.

"You don't belong here," he shouted before turning to run.

"Then I won't belong anywhere," August answered back in a voice only I could here.

Since the exchange between August and Wesley had effectively cleared out what remained of the patrons, I decided to close the bar early and go with August to search for my mother and Nahil.

We had just put away the last of the dirty dishes when we heard a noise in the back yard that turned out to be my mother creeping through the alley on the way to our back door. In her arms, she carried two bags and my brother, who was wrapped around her arms and waist like a toddler.

I ran down the stairs to meet her. "Maji, where were you?" I scolded. "What are you doing out here so late? We were just about to go looking for you!"

Because the light was fading, I couldn't see her face clearly until she stepped closer to the lantern that we kept burning on the back porch, but the moment I did, I wished that I had kept all my questions to myself.

Despite the way her head was buried in Nahil's thick hair, I could see that her face was tear-strained and drawn with exhaustion. Her bright green sari was torn and dirty with streaks of dried mud from the sleeves of her dress to the bottom of her skirt. At the crease of her arms the bags from her trip to the market left angry marks that were already bruised, swollen or bleeding.

Tears filled my eyes as I tried not to imagine all the things that must have occurred to bring my mother, the most dignified woman I had ever known, to such a state.

"Maji, are you alright? I'm so sorry. Are you hurt? Who hurt you, Maji?" I babbled, but my mother could only shake her head in response as new tears began to fall.

August tried to lift Nahil from her as I guided her to the stairs, but he would not let go. That's when I realized that he was crying, too.

"Shhh, Nahil. Be still for Maji. I'm here. We're almost home now," she whispered and I wondered how long she'd been uttering those words to him.

When removing Nahil proved impossible, my mother shifted her arms so that August could take her bags from her arms. With more of the bruises showing, I knew that removing the bags must have stung her, but she said nothing.

August carried our groceries while I lifted her sari enough to guide her into the kitchen safely. Once inside, we locked the door and settled them into the small table and chair that we used for cutting vegetables.

"Please, Ma," I began. "Tell us what happened."

August brought a glass of water and set it down beside her before disappearing somewhere behind me. In the back of my mind, I was aware that he was strangely quiet, but in that moment, I couldn't focus on anything other than my family.

"I think Nahil is finally sleeping. Check for me. I want to make sure before I tell you."

Looking over my mother's shoulder, Nahil's mud-stained face looked peaceful, despite whatever trauma he'd endured. Slowly, I eased him from my mother's arms and onto my lap as I waited.

After a sip of water and a nod of thanks to August, she began to tell us where she had been.

"The market was very crowded today, more crowded than I can remember seeing it. We were almost through with our shopping when we heard a commotion. At first, we couldn't tell what it was or where it was coming from, but as the crowd began to clear, I could see them—two men, running from several British officers. One of the men who was trying to escape tripped on a basket in the aisle. The other man went back to help him, but by that time, the officers had caught up to them.

"I realized what was happening too late to shield Nahil from it. The officers beat those men so brutally, right there in the market in front of all of us—called them traitors. There were so many people all frozen in place so that I couldn't move, couldn't get away before they brought the ropes. They hung them right there in the street and told us all that this is what would happen to anyone who helped those who rebelled against the Company. Nahil kept crying. I tried to keep him from looking, but he still saw too much, more than any child should see. After that, the officers started questioning people, grabbing them from their stalls, opening their bags and throwing their things on the ground.

"People began to run. Nahil and I ran, too, but together, we couldn't keep up. I tried to avoid the main roads, keep to the alleys. It was chaos. There was no reason to whom they stopped or why. They just wanted to prove that we had no rights, that they controlled us. All around I heard the sounds of women, men and children screaming. I didn't know what they would do if they found us, so we just kept running. After a while, Nahil became so upset. He wouldn't run anymore. He just kept crying for your father. I couldn't find a rickshaw to bring us home, so I walked with him in my arms most of the way."

When she'd finished, I was speechless, overcome with gratitude for the strength she found to endure all that she had and make it home.

"I'm sorry, Maji. I should have closed the bar and come looking for you earlier."

"No!" my mother said, visibly shaken. "I didn't want you out there with those men. With each step I took, I prayed that you were safe at home." Looking up at August, she continued. "I prayed that you were here and that you would be able to protect my daughter."

"Mrs. Masir, I'm not sure I had anything to do with Satish's safety, but with your permission, I would like to be here to ensure your family's safety for as long as you will allow me."

I held my breath, waiting for my mother's response as she looked between us, with sadness and resignation warring in her eyes.

Finally, she let out a long sigh.

"We would be grateful for any help you can provide. Satish can make room for you in the kitchen or in the dining hall if you like."

"Please, you needn't go through any trouble. I'll be fine with one of the chairs from the bar."

"Please, Lt. Mortimer, you are our guest. Satish will find you a blanket and pillow to make you more comfortable."

With effort, my mother rose to her feet and motioned for me to hand her Nahil.

"I'll carry him, Ma. Go on."

"Goodnight then," she nodded before heading for the stairs.

"Good evening," August said before turning to me. "I need to get my gun and a few more supplies from my flat. I'll be back in fifteen minutes."

The look on my face must have given all my fear away, because he leaned down then and kissed my forehead before returning his gaze to mine.

"Fifteen minutes. I promise."

I nodded and watched as he headed out the back door.

It took me almost an hour to get my mother bathed and settled in. She was more affected by her ordeal than I realized, and as I tended to her cuts and bruises, I gained a new respect for everything she had gone through to return to me.

I took extra time braiding her hair and oiling her body, trying to show her how much I loved her and appreciated her trust in me and by extension, August. She sat so quietly through most of my ministrations that I thought at times that she had simply fallen asleep. So I dressed her for bed in silence, but as I laid her down next to Nahil, she grabbed my arm with surprising force.

"You are not married, yet! I have given no permission. Do you understand me, Satish. I will not sell you at any price!"

Her nails dug into my skin, but I did not protest. I knew my mother was only trying to hold on to everything she feared to lose.

"I understand, Maji. I promise," I whispered, patting the fingers that gripped me. She looked into my eyes for a long time until she found what she was looking for, then closed her eyes and let me go.

By the time I reached downstairs, August had locked and barricaded all the doors.

I smiled.

He said he'd only gone for a few things, but by the two sacks of clothes I saw tucked into the corner, it looked like he had every intention of settling in, which was fine by me.

I turned away from him, my arms full of sheets and blankets, and made a bed out of the booth at the back of the restaurant. The feel of him watching me as I worked was electric, but I didn't realize that he was so close until I'd finished my work and felt his hands settle on my shoulders.

"Thank you," he said softly as I turned to face him.

"My mother thinks that we . . . us," I paused to point a finger back and forth "are a bad idea."

August looked at me incredulously. "We are a bad idea. I'm sure your mother and mine would agree." Then his smile dropped. "Does it matter to you, Satish, what she thinks?"

Then, it was my turn to look at him as if he had said something stupid. "Obviously not. I just made your bed. Why? Does it matter to you?"

"Not a bit," he said before leaning down to kiss me. I pulled away breathless, then ran upstairs with the silliest grin spread all over my face.

I woke up to the faint sound of bells ringing from The Flagstaff Tower, signaling that the city was under attack. The soldiers from Meerut are here, I thought, as a shiver ran down my spine. I dressed quickly and ran downstairs, planning to wake August and find out what we might expect for the day. My eyes went first to the back of the room, to the bed I'd made for him, but aside from the skewed angle of the pillow, the blankets looked barely touched.

For a brief second, I panicked, frightened by the ominous dark of the room and the thought that he'd left sometime during the night. But then my eyes adjusted enough for me to make out his slim frame, standing less than ten feet from where I'd left him last night, with his rifle propped up at his side. By the look on August's face when he turned toward me, it seemed like he'd been up all night.

His eyes were tired as he took me in.

"Don't open the café today," he said softly. "If this day goes the way I think it will, it won't be safe for you."

I walked up behind him and wrapped my arms around his chest, pressing my cheek into the space between his shoulder blades. Just the smell of him calmed me.

His fingers intertwined with mine for a moment before turning around in my arms.

"Where are my manners? This is the first time I'm getting to see you by the first light of day. Good morning, Satish. How did you sleep?"

"Better than you, I think. Mother and Nahil are still asleep. Mother never sleeps late; they must be exhausted from yesterday."

"They should be, and I don't think it's going to get any better today."

"Do you really think we should close the bar? All day?"

"Absolutely, I think the only people who would come here today are the wrong kind of customers. If the sepoys attack, the British will be brutal, Satish. Trust me on this."

Just as he finished, we heard someone pounding on the back door.

August picked up his gun and ran to the kitchen.

"Don't," I hissed from behind him. "It's probably just Mahood and Guna."

"Then why are they knocking," August insisted.

Looking at the clock, I couldn't believe the time. "Because it's a quarter to seven in the morning, and the door is usually wide open by now."

August lowered the gun slightly as if considering something before motioning for me to come a bit closer. Then he whispered in my ear, "Ask who is it."

I did as he asked and listened to the quivering voice that returned.

"Satish? Satish? It's us. Please let us in," the voice sounded a lot like Guna's but I couldn't be sure."

August shook his head "no", but I persisted.

"Who is 'us'?"

"It's Guna, Satish. And Mahood. We came here alone to make sure you were alright. We promised your father we would look out for you."

Slowly, August made his way to the door, removing the various barricades that he had put together the night before. Slowly, he unlocked the door and cracked it open for me to see.

The look of disbelief on Mahood and Guna's faces when August and I appeared in the doorway was something I will never forget.

I almost had to convince them to come in despite the fact that they had been climbing these back steps every day for over a decade.

Guna approached me first, placing both hands on my shoulders as he tried to lead me out of the kitchen. If he saw August twitch with discomfort, he didn't let it show.

"What is he doing here, Satish?" Guna asked. "Do you know what has happened? Where is your mother?"

"Mother is upstairs sleeping," I said while shrugging him off. "And yes, I do know what's going on out there."

He looked at me, unconvinced. "The British and the sepoys have begun killing people. Yesterday, it was just the British in the market place. Today, it's the British and the sepoys. The sepoys have already tried to petition the Emperor."

August put his gun down and stepped forward. "When? This morning?"

"Yes," Mahood answered warily. "He has not given them a private audience yet, but who knows what will happen now?" As August turned away deep in thought, Mahood turned his attention back to me. "Please, Satish, don't open the bar today. There is too much danger nearby."

"So everyone keeps telling me," I answered, just as my mother walked fully dressed into the kitchen.

Mahood and Guna left shortly after, but returned several times throughout the morning, bringing news of the day— the mass hanging of sepoys by the British, the killing of shop owners, Indian Christians, and European soldiers by sepoys who condemned them as "British sympathizers". The violence was escalating, but no one seemed to have the upper hand, they reported.

For most of the morning and into the afternoon, my mother and I ate little and cleaned far too much, while August lifted things too heavy for us to move in between pacing like a wild animal in a cage. Nahil had yet to come down, despite our best efforts. I could hear his toys scraping lightly across the floor above us as we cleaned, and while it seemed to put everyone else on edge, the knowledge that someone I loved was able to shut themselves off from the world around us comforted me.

After bringing Nahil a cold samosa from the icebox, I came down the stairs to see August checking his gun for the third time in what had to be less than twenty minutes.

"You should go with Mahood and Guna the next time they come," I said finally. "You can come back and check on us later."

August sighed as he peaked out from the drawn curtains. "Things will only get worse, Satish. If I left now, by the time I return, it might be too late to get you out."

While I stood still, confused about what he meant, my mother stopped pretending to ignore our conversation and stood up from where she had been dusting the baseboards near the front door.

"Do you think it will come to that, Lt. Mortimer?"

"Yes, madam. I'm sorry to say it, but I believe it will, quickly."

Mother dropped her polishing cloth on a nearby table and began wringing her hands.

"Where would we go? We have no family left. This was our home, with my husband . . ."

"I'm sorry," August said as he stepped towards her. "I am sorry for your loss, truly I am, but . . . you are from the north, are you not? The Kashmir region, if I'm not mistaken."

"Yes," my mother replied cautiously. "I have an aunt there, but I have not seen her in many years . . ."

"I've been trying to come up with a plan to secure your passage there, but I will need to find a sepoy soldier that I can trust. He will also need to trust me and not hold your association with me against you. With British soldiers now willing to kill their own sepoy troops, as Guna reported last, that will not be easy."

"How could they do that, kill the men who have served them loyally for all these years?"

"I do not know," August answered, "but we are on the brink of war, and I fear that honor will not be a factor in it."

"How would you secure our passage?"

"I asked Mahood to find an officer that used to be under my command and give him a message. If he agrees to help us, he will be here at 6pm this evening with a carriage and some provisions to take you to your family. If not, I am working on a plan to get you out myself, but travelling with me may not be safe."

Mother's eyes were wide as she started to ask more questions, but she quieted quickly as Nahil crept downstairs.

"Can I have a honey cake, please?" he asked sweetly, looking from my mother to me as the first hint of a smile crossed his face.

My mother took only one step towards him before a deafening explosion shook the ground, sending shards of glass exploding all around us.

※

I woke up to an uncommon sound—for once the world was silent, aside from a faint, distant ringing in my ear. I felt weightless floating through air that was as grey as a cloud. And for a moment, I didn't have a care in the world. Then I heard my mother scream.

My world rushed back to me as all my senses rallied to find the source of my mother's pain. It hurt to turn my head, but I did. I saw a shirt that was torn and stained with blood. I looked up to find August's face, his jaw firm and eyes set on his destination. He was taking me upstairs.

"What—" I began, then gagged on the dust in my mouth. "What's happened?"

"I don't know, an explosion of some kind, I think coming from the arsenal, most likely. I need to go and check it out, but first I need to set your brother's arm. It's broken."

I tried to shift my weight, twist my body so that I could get down and rush back to Nahil, but a terrible pain in my left leg took my breath away.

"Don't!" August said looking down at me. I could see a large red gash along the right side of his face from his temple all the way down to his jaw.

"You have a cut on your leg that was bleeding very badly. I managed to stop the bleeding, but any sudden movements could open it. Be still, Satish, or you'll die."

"Will my brother . . . ?" The tears stung my eyes.

"No, it's a clean break. I think he'll be fine. I just have to set it."

"Do you know how?" I asked as he put me down on our bed and arranged the blankets over me.

"Yes," he said with a small smile in his eyes. "I broke a lot bones falling out of trees as a boy. Every time the doctors patched me up, I watched and learned. I had wanted to be a physician before . . . before this."

Though I wanted to focus, to know more, my head ached terribly, and I felt slightly nauseated. He seemed to sense my discomfort and lifted my head to give me a small sip of water.

"Try to rest and lie very still. I need to get back to your brother. Your mother is beside herself."

I don't remember him leaving, but when I opened my eyes again, my brother and my mother were beside me. Nahil had what looked like broken slats of smooth wood tied to his forearm with strips from the bed sheets I'd laid out for August.

My leg stung and throbbed so badly that I was afraid to even lift my head to look at it. Unable to move, I listened for any hint of August downstairs, but all I could hear were faint cries from the street below and the sound of gunfire in the distance. It wasn't dark yet, so I couldn't see the fire, but I could smell the smoke in the air.

I didn't hear the sound of footsteps on the stairs, so when the floorboards of our bedroom creaked, I almost screamed.

"Shh, Satish, it's me, Guna. Don't be afraid." Guna raised the lantern he was holding so that I could see his kind face for myself. "I brought you some of your mother's tea, to fight infection. He said I had to hold your head and feed it to you, so that you didn't move. Do you mind?"

I nodded my consent and thanked him. In between sips, I tried to put the pieces of what happened together.

I started with the most important detail first.

"Where is he, Lt. Mortimer?"

"He left once your mother and Nahil were settled. By the time I got here, he was already patching Nahil's arm. He made me promise to carry this gun around with me everywhere I went while I was with you."

A knot settled in my stomach as I thought of him, unarmed on bloodstained streets. Then another thought occurred to me.

"Where is Mahood? Has he returned?"

Guna looked away and I knew without him saying the words.

"What time is it, now?" Guna looked back at me, but the sadness only deepened.

"Half-past seven, Satish, and the Lieutenant has not returned. It's been more than two hours now. He said if he did not come back by morning that I should find a carriage to take you north myself. He left money for passage."

My throat was suddenly raw as I thought of all the things conspiring against us.

What if, he'd asked me only two nights ago. My tears were breaking and welling again with the certainty that we would never know.

"Drink your tea, Satish. Please. He may still come. He's only a little bit late. An hour at the most."

※

I lay in the dark listening to the sound of my own breathing, the screams that had only gotten louder with the setting of the sun, the crackle of fires burning, and the clip clop of horses racing by. I could feel the chaos closing in around us, but even then, I tuned it out. My mind reached out, listening for the stillness in the cacophony of sound that only two careful feet would make. Two feet that would hide in shadows to go unnoticed, so that no one would follow him, so that no one would be drawn back to our location.

I knew instinctively that these feet would sound completely different from the shuffle Guna made downstairs as he carried his gun back and forth, unsure of what he could do if he had to use it. Guna was a fine waiter, the best my father ever trained, but he was no soldier. Still, he knew honor, loyalty, and duty, things that set him apart and made him a better guard than more physically able men.

But I sought past him, pushing away his sounds and all the others the dark could make until I found what I was looking for in the slight creak of our back door and the quick stride that would erase the distance between us in seconds.

Before he spoke to Guna, August's feet were on the steps.

"Are they ready, Guna? Load the bags while I bring them down. There's no time."

The next thing I knew, he was crossing into our bedroom in a tattered officer's jacket with a lantern held high in one hand and a pristine white handkerchief clutched in the other.

His face was unreadable as he looked from me to my mother, then spoke.

"I'm sorry, Mrs. Masir, but we must make haste. All the carriages are leaving. I've secured your passage, but we must leave now."

My mother, who I assumed was sleeping during my vigil, sprung out of the bed immediately. I noticed then that she was fully dressed.

"Yes. Thank you, Lieutenant. We're already packed."

August moved aside so that my mother could pass, then reached down and picked up Nahil and carried him downstairs.

My heart pounded as I tried to think, tried to put the pieces together.

Before I could begin to make sense of anything, August had returned and kneeled down beside me.

"I don't understand," I whispered, searching his eyes for anything kinder than the truth. The mask of his face fell as he leaned forward and crushed his lips to mine.

"I wanted more time," he murmured back. "I wanted so much more time with you."

"August, what is happening?"

His pale grey eyes looked dark as he stared back at me. I knew we had so much to say to each other and no time left to say it.

"I'm taking you away from here, someplace safe. Brace yourself."

Before I could ask, I found out what he meant. My thigh seemed to ignite as he lifted me, burning and stinging and stretching all at once. I wanted to faint, but instead I clutched on to his jacket and clenched my teeth together to stop myself from screaming. I was shaking and covered with sweat by the time he brought me to the wagon. Inside were the blankets from his makeshift bed and a pillow from one of the bar couches. Nahil, my mother and Guna sat beside me as I lay panting on my back, trying not to cry as August mounted the horse that pulled us. As we raced through the streets, all I remember was the sound of his whip as smoke from the city filled the sky.

The wagon stopped within a flurry of commotion and panic as carriages and horses rustled and bucked in a mad effort to escape what was coming.

"The sepoys are coming!" someone yelled from a tower. "The sepoys are coming!"

To my right, my mother looked more terrified than I had ever seen her before as she clutched Nahil to her and looked around. On my back, I couldn't see much aside from the backsides of horses and the tops of fine carriages—the kind of carriages that only the British or Indian nobility could afford.

Guna looked completely out of sorts as he helped Mother and Nahil out of the wagon, but I didn't fully understand until August came around and lifted me into his arms.

"Guna, it's the black carriage to the left. Lead them," he said in a rush as he strode purposefully behind.

An eerie silence descended as we walked through the crowd, the only Indians in a sea of British soldiers and their families. Children stared and women gaped, incredulous, while soldiers narrowed their eyes in contempt.

"August, this isn't going to work. We don't belong here," I whispered.

"Just hold on to me, Satish. This has to work. It's the only way."

My fingernails dug into his collar as I tried to match his resolve and meet each stare that followed us.

We reached the carriage faster than expected, no doubt thanks to the crowd that parted for us as if we were lepers.

With my mother's help, August settled me into the carriage and propped my leg up with a box that lay on the floor so that it would be straight for the duration of our journey.

For a moment, August looked around the carriage before his eyes settled on me.

"The roads will be bad, so try your best to stay as still as you can. Your mother knows how to change the bandages, so . . ." His voice trailed off as he looked down then took my hand.

"You're not coming with us." I couldn't say it louder than a whisper.

Behind him, an irate man in full officer regalia was pointing at August and coming closer, but I couldn't find it in myself to care. Nothing that man had to say could be worse than what I already knew.

"Lt. Mortimer!" the man yelled.

August looked up then, and there he was, the shy, awkward man from those first nights at the bar all over again.

"Would you keep something for me until we see each other again? A token of my love, of my intentions . . ."

I watched as he reached in and pulled a white handkerchief from his breast pocket.

"Lt. Mortimer!"

The fine cloth was trimmed on each side with the finest lace I'd ever seen. On the farthest corner the initials A.M. were stitched in a bright blue that matched the stone inside.

The ring was set in gold, with diamonds surrounding a deep blue stone that stood slightly elevated from the rest. He picked it up gently and held my fingers open.

"Lt. Mortimer! This is completely unacceptable!"

"It was my grandmother's," he said calmly. "You know I was closer to her than anyone, even my own mother. She understood me. She gave this to me a long time ago and told me to give it to the woman who helped me feel less lost in this world. She told me to give it to the woman I wanted to marry."

He looked up at me then, with eyes smiling despite the chaos and fire around us. He was himself again. He was himself with me.

"Would you keep this for me, Satish? Would you do me this honor?"

His hand held out the ring, just above my fingertip.

"Lt. Mortimer! I am your superior! I demand you turn around this instant!"

"Yes," I whispered back, joy dissolving so easily with the tears and sorrow. "I will keep it until you come to take its place."

His smile was broad and true, despite every reason not to be, and my heart swelled past the hopelessness that surrounded us to something greater—the truth of who we are.

I leaned in and kissed him as deeply as I knew how.

"I love you, August. I love you."

"As I love you, Sa—"

The awful man put his hand on August's shoulder and yanked him around. I would have screamed, except the foreignness of August's voice stunned me into silence. I imagined in that moment that he sounded more British than the Queen of England herself.

"What the devil are you doing, Harold? Can't you see I'm saying goodbye to my wife!"

The man looked red as a beet against the blue of his uniform, with sweat pooling and dripping around the brim of his ridiculous white hat.

"Your what! Have you lost your mind? These carriages are reserved for British officers and their families!"

"I am a British officer, am I not? And this is my family," August stepped aside and lifted my hand. "Captain Archer, may I introduce to you my new bride, Mrs. August Mortimer, my mother in-law Mrs. Masir and her son, Nahil, who is of course now my brother-in-law. I'm sending them to Kashmir to wait for me until all this ugly business is sorted out."

The man turned so red with shock that I thought he would faint. I shared his sentiment, but I dared not let it show. I put on my best smile and tried to assume my new position, even though it was less than a minute old.

"How do you do?" I said politely and bowed my head gently, like I'd seen British women do at the bar sometimes. I always thought they looked like donkeys, but now, with our lives on the line, I desperately hoped I looked the same. It must have worked because the red officer looked from the ring on my finger to my face as if the two could not possibly exist together. When my smile widened, he looked away.

"For God's sake, August, we're at war and you go and . . ." August's demeanor didn't slip, but if you looked closely, his smug smile was leaning more and more towards a sneer. August cut Harold off, just in time.

"Quite right, Harold! We are at war, so we'd better get this over with and let the women and children be on their way. As poor Edmund keeps trying to tell us from the tower up there, the sepoys are coming."

This seemed to snap the red officer back to the issue at hand.

"I can not argue with you there, August. I suppose we will discuss your nuptials at a more appropriate time." Turning to me, he continued. "Good day and safe travels, eh, madam." He nodded curtly and turned to leave before looking back. "I'll see you at the front line, Mortimer."

"Right next to you, Harold. Right next to you!" August answered and waved him along as if he was without a care in the world.

"The front line!" I hissed before a loud explosion shook the ground.

"You need to leave!" It was his only reply as he closed the carriage door then reached in to cradle my face in his hands. He kissed me one last time, then let me go.

"August!" I shouted over the horses and the carriages pounding by.

"मै तुमसे प्यार करता हूँ" I love you, he replied, then locked the door.

"Go, and don't let that gun out of your sight! Don't stop for anything, not until sunrise." He was speaking to Guna, but looking straight at me. He stepped away and hit the side of the carriage twice, watching as the horses took off and carried us away.

If I could have jumped from the carriage, I would have, but my mother's arms were strong, and August had locked the door from the outside, which I was too beside myself to realize until it was too late.

And so I watched as he joined the pitiful line of men who stood with guns raised against men who rushed in like a storm swelling up from the dust below. I saw the first of the British soldiers fall before explosion after explosion set the line of men ablaze.

There were never enough of them to win, nor was that their intention. They were only there to ensure safe passage for those they loved, to pay the price of a carriage.

I imagined August screaming in pain from fire, a gunshot or some other horrible death, and I screamed with him. Oh, how I screamed. But I knew he couldn't hear me. Not anymore.

Part III

Code Talker
December 7, 1941 ~ Oahu, Hawaii

She woke up to find herself face down in the dirt. Though she couldn't remember where she was or how she got there, instinct told her to take inventory. The right side of her face burned, but she was fairly sure she wasn't on fire. She would have recognized the scent of burning flesh. The pain in her shoulder told her that rolling to her left was impossible, so she dug her opposite hand into the ground, searching for the leverage to push her body upward. That's when she saw the blood and torn flesh of her hands. Ignoring the pain, she continued to push, lifting her upper body into a semi-upright position. Anticipating what would come next, she squeezed her eyes shut against the wave of dizziness and nausea that followed.

What is your name? she asked herself silently, pulling her knees up under her and shifting her hips to the side. Her body trembled from the effort, but she was pleased that she managed to get into a sitting position. Nothing seemed broken. She took a deep breath and tried again. What is your name?

Anna, she thought with profound relief. My name is Anna Rose Freeman.

The simple knowledge was euphoric. She could move, and she knew her name. The rest would come later.

I'm okay. Keep moving, Anna told herself as she brought her knees in closer, preparing to stand. But she didn't make it far before she heard commotion from behind—shouting and the pounding of feet coming quickly.

"彼女をゲット！彼女をゲット！"

The language was not her own, but she understood it perfectly. *Get her! Get her!*

Awareness came in a rush. Ignoring the pain that pressed in from every corner of her body, Anna scrambled to her feet and ran.

"彼女の距離を取得させてはいけません！" *Don't let her get away!*

Anna thought she could make out two distinct male voices, but didn't dare turn around to see.

Her legs moved with a strength and speed that surprised her, but the men were closer than she realized, and before she could hit her stride, she was back on the ground, this time with someone twice her weight on her back. Anna screamed in agony as her assailant brought her arms up and over her head roughly, but the pain brought a strange relief too as her shoulder popped back into its socket. When the soldier finished patting her body down, he turned her over.

For a moment, they both stared at each other in shock. Panic set in as his face unlocked the missing pieces of who and where she was.

What is he doing here? She tried to remember if they'd received any warning of an attack. But there was nothing in her memory that could explain the presence of a young Japanese soldier on the island of Oahu, at an American Naval Base in Pearl Harbor.

His gaze was far less calculating than hers as his eyes took in her every feature. For a moment, his fascination seemed to distract him from his duties as he fumbled to bind her hands. The soldier even had the humility to look slightly embarrassed when Anna caught him rubbing his thumbs over the skin on her wrists unnecessarily. But he hid it well, mostly.

Then the reason dawned on her. *I'm probably the first Black person he's ever seen.* Anna started to ask what he wanted and why he was here in the language he would understand, but then she caught herself.

They can't know. No one can know, she reminded herself.

"彼女はここで何をしているのですか？" *What is she doing here?*

The voice that asked the question came from someone she couldn't see. Someone who was standing just beyond her field of sight. The soldier finished binding her legs before giving an answer.

"関係ない。キャプテン山本は茂みに脱出しようとしている別のものを見つけました。行きましょう。" *Doesn't matter. Captain Yamamoto found another one trying to escape in the bushes. Let's go.*

As if to emphasize his point, the soldier yanked Anna up into a sitting position. Without the pain in her shoulder, Anna took in her surroundings for the first time. Buildings burned all around her. Splintered trunks of the palm trees she had grown to love were reduced to blackened bark, and just beyond their ruined beauty stood the harbor, strewn with bodies. The USS Arizona, the ship that she would have called home for almost 3 months, loomed against the sky like a twisted monster, breathing black smoke and flame as it devoured the men she could hear still screaming inside.

But there was nothing she could do for them now but keep their secret.

Suddenly, Anna's vision narrowed as the dizziness returned. Annoyed by the distraction of what she dismissed as only a minor concussion, Anna pressed her eyes shut and fought against the haze that lingered at the edges of her consciousness.

Stay alert. You can't afford to make a mistake and give something away. Remember who you are! Anna commanded, even as she felt herself slipping farther away. It was the last thought she remembered before something else took hold.

The officer pulled Anna to her feet. And that's when she saw him, the other man to whom the soldier had been speaking all this time.

Relief washed over her. His features, his dress, even his language were all wrong, and yet she knew exactly who he was.

"Ekow! Ekow, upendo wangu!" Ekow! Ekow, my love! she exclaimed, moving towards him despite the bindings at her ankles.

The stranger she knew stared back at her in confusion, then stepped away from her advance.

The move stung her deeply, even though some part of her was aware that it should not have—the same part that told her that she didn't know him any more than he knew her. But the assertion in her thoughts caused a revolt in her body. The nausea hit stronger this time, coupled with a shooting pain at the left side of her skull. Anna instinctively reached out for something to hold onto as her knees began to buckle. The second man who had backed away only seconds before suddenly lunged forward to catch her before she hit the ground.

The first soldier narrowed his eyes in immediate suspicion.

"あなたはこの女性を知っていますか？" *Do you know this woman?*

Before she could wonder how she'd ended up in his arms, Anna turned away sharply, terrified of the answer he would give. Did he know her secret? Would he give it away? The answers seemed too far for her to grasp. The threads of her consciousness were unraveling quickly and she couldn't follow or remember anything that had just happened.

I don't know him; he doesn't know me. He couldn't. He couldn't, Anna tried to reassure herself.

"私は私の人生の中で前に彼女を見たことがありません。どのように私は彼女が誰であるか知っているだろうか？" *Sato, I have never seen her before in my life. How could I know who she is?*

The words should have filled her with relief, but instead, tears pricked her eyes, as she absorbed the pain of his denial. In protest, Anna tried to stand and push him away, but it was no use. Her eyes fell closed as the tears ran down her face and she slipped into unconsciousness.

※

Why did I do that?

Commander Ichiro Oimikado didn't remember making the decision to catch her, he just did. He told himself that his actions were only good training, the mark of a gentleman, as his British colleagues in medical school would have said, to assist a woman in need. But these were not genteel times. He was a man at war and she was his enemy.

The incident happened hours ago, yet he couldn't get it out of his mind. Ichiro also couldn't shake the strange charge that coursed through his body ever since he had touched her. His unit had already transported the prisoners back to their base on Hiroshima and was preparing to perform full medical assessments before interrogation began in the morning.

When he'd ordered separate quarters for her, most had assumed that it was because she was their only female prisoner. Only Private Sato tried to rouse suspicion, but his attempts to disparage Ichiro were useless. Ichiro's family name and rank in the Imperial Navy were beyond reproach. He came from a distinguished family with a long history of ties to the Emperor. No one questioned his motives.

Except, Ichiro knew that despite Private Sato's jealousies, his instincts had been right. He had placed their female prisoner in the medical wing not because she was female, but because there he had the greatest authority to watch over her.

The thought that he would desire to do such a thing was deeply disturbing. He had given up his schooling, a promising medical career, and postponed his marriage to Naoko to perform his duty, to forsake everything he knew to be true about Germany to save his country from starvation and honor his commitment to his family. That he could have any sympathy towards a prisoner at all was treason. That he could feel the need to protect his country's worst enemy was beyond anything he could logically fathom, but he did feel the need—intensely.

Once back in his office, Ichiro closed the door and unbuttoned his jacket before sinking down into his chair. Beside his desk was a large window that looked out onto the place where the Honkawa and Motoyasu Rivers parted ways. A mist had blown in from the

Chogoku Mountains, cloaking the city in a billowy pale grey fog. But as he turned towards the view, he could see nothing but her face calling out to him in a language he didn't know, but understood nonetheless.

Ekow! Ekow, upendo wangu!

Looking into the mist, Ichiro dissected the memory. It was the expression on her face, he told himself, terror broken by blinding hope, and her outstretched hand that made him understand.

She had called out to me, not as a stranger, but as someone she knew and trusted. She had called me Ekow. Ichiro wasn't sure how he knew this, but he was sure of it.

At the time, the familiarity of it startled him, like the burden lifted when you finally recall a word that has lingered just out of memory's reach.

It didn't make any sense, but if that were all, he would have thought of it as no more than a curious encounter, something to pick apart and study like his medical journals, but that wasn't all. In the moment that she had called out to him, he had been ready to say, "Yes" to anything she asked. He'd been about to do it, would have done it had he not caught sight of Private Sato.

The look of reproach from Private Sato was like a sound slap in the face. It brought him back to the moment and the very real situation they were in as enemy invaders in the middle of hostile territory.

A flash of panic came over him. What am I doing?

He'd stepped away from her then, trying to free himself from the pull he felt and immediately saw the hurt burning in her eyes. It should not have affected him. His response should not have affected her either, but then, she began to fall.

Ichiro shuddered as he recalled the word he heard then, coming from a place that had no voice until he touched her. As he caught her in his arms, a word he'd never heard before pressed itself into the forefront of his mind.

A word.

A name.

He watched the tears roll down her face as consciousness left her and he knew, without a doubt, that her name was Ama.

※

Ichiro carried her back to the small carrier plane himself. No one questioned him because he was taller and stronger than most of the men around him, but the truth was that it didn't take a particularly strong man to lift her. Ichiro did it because he didn't want anyone else to. When he strapped her into the co-pilot seat beside him, no one uttered a word. They were all silently fascinated by the strange woman they never expected to capture on this island, and Ichiro used their distraction to set things in motion the way he wanted them.

Ichiro kept all thoughts of what he was doing and why he was doing it at bay until he got her back to his examination room. Though Ichiro had planned to specialize in psychology, he had completed his basic medical training at the University of London. His training and rank gave him authority over the base's medical operations, so it was not unusual that he would conduct a medical examination himself. It was only after all the arrangements were made, when he was finally alone with her, that Ichiro began to face the implications of what he had done.

As if watching himself from afar, he cataloged the emotions of possession and attraction that coursed through him as he went through his examination. He had always been focused and passionate about his work, but this was different. The woman on the gurney in front of him was a stranger to him in every practical way. He had no reason to care for her, yet he could feel a growing compulsion to be near her, to hear her voice, to see her open her eyes and know that she was unharmed. Though her features were different from any other woman he had known, he found her exceptionally beautiful. But he could not explain his actions away as mere attraction. The feeling inside him was more akin to necessity than lust, which made him all the more afraid.

The fact that she had not regained consciousness since they left Pearl Harbor concerned him, but as he treated the various bruises and injuries she'd sustained in the attack, he could understand why.

Sharing his diagnosis of a severe concussion with the medical team, he ordered 24-hour surveillance of their only female prisoner, so that when she woke up, they could record any helpful information she might provide. To be effective, the surveillance had to be conducted by the only three officers on the base who spoke English. Ichiro was, of course, one of them. The other two officers were Commander Fukigama, who almost never left their translation unit, and Private Sato.

So as not to arouse suspicion, he allowed Private Sato to take the first shift, noting that it would be extremely unlikely that she would wake within the next 12 hours. If he was right, when she did wake up, Ichiro would be the first person she saw, which was exactly how he wanted it.

The first thing Anna sensed when she woke up was the bandage wrapped firmly around her head. The second thing was the smell. It was clean and light, like lemons and fresh air—except for the hint of something antiseptic.

Alcohol!

Startled, Anna sat up in the bed to find herself hand-cuffed to it by her right wrist. The second thing she noted was the lack of windows and the absolute stillness of the room. Once again, she had no idea of where she was or how she had gotten there. But as she looked around at the glass medicine cabinets and empty medical beds, the memory of the USS Arizona and the curious eyes of the soldier who bound her wrists together slowly came back to her.

The attack . . . they've taken me prisoner.

Anna suppressed the shudder that tried to make its way through her body and took a deep breath.

Don't panic. Think! You've been trained for this, she reminded herself. There was a dull ache that throbbed in her left temple, but other than that, she felt well enough.

If I can move, I can get out of here, she told herself while shrugging her shoulders to test them. The pain was nothing she couldn't handle. Feeling a little more focused, Anna shifted her forearm to examine the lock on her handcuffs for a moment before reaching into the twists of her hair for a bobby pin.

She had just inserted the pin into the handcuff lock when a voice from behind made her jump.

"Good morning, or should I say, good evening. I'm glad you are feeling well enough to escape."

The accent was thick, but his pronunciation was perfect. Anna twisted her body around so that she could get a look at the man who had startled her.

In a corner, behind a small recess in the wall, he sat.

How long has he been sitting there watching me? I didn't even hear him breathing.

Though her memory of the man who had bound her hands was not clear, she was sure she had never seen this man before. Since she had already been caught trying to escape, Anna decided there was no need to be coy. "What do you want? Release me, immediately!" She demanded.

The man before her smiled, a small, pleasant smile that seemed warm and sincere despite the circumstances.

"If I had given you a few moments more, I think you might have been able to accomplish that yourself. It would have been interesting to see how you did, but then we would have missed the chance to be formally introduced. I am Commander Ichiro Oimikado of the Imperial Navy. And you are . . . ?"

The man before her extended his hand as if to shake hers before seemingly thinking better of it. Instead, he turned to a small table beside him and poured her a glass of water. If he had been coarse or cruel, Anna would have been better prepared, but he was cautiously cordial and disarmingly handsome. He even had a sense of humor. Anna looked at him and the glass of water warily and said nothing.

Understanding her reservations, Ichiro took a small sip of water, before handing it to her, making sure that their fingers did not touch. He let her finish the water before speaking.

"Please, I'm sure you have many questions, and I would like to answer them, but first I would like to know your name. It can't be much of a risk to tell me that, can it?"

His tone was light, but his eyes were serious. She'd already made one mistake in front of him; she couldn't afford another.

He's testing me, she realized. Would there be any harm in telling him my name? If I were anyone else, any other prisoner would not hesitate to give as much. There were only five people who knew who she really was and none of them were on Oahu.

"My name is Anna. Anna Freeman," she said finally.

For some reason she couldn't imagine, he seemed surprised, almost as if he expected her to say something else.

"Anna, you say," he answered, putting special emphasis on the 'n'. He opened up a small notebook that fit in the palm of his hand and began to write.

"Yes," she replied, as she tried to get a glimpse of what he was writing.

"Well, then, it's good that you remember it. You took a pretty bad fall during our attack. You were unconscious for almost 48 hours. It's a good sign that perhaps you haven't suffered any permanent brain damage." He smiled again, but this time there was no warmth in it. Anna wondered what had changed, then decided that she didn't care. The time for pleasantries was over.

"You said you would answer my questions. Where am I and what do you want with me?"

Standing smoothly, he stepped a fraction closer to her before answering.

"You, Ms. Freeman, are in the Empire of Japan. You are our prisoner here along with three more of your countrymen, and we are looking for the code talker."

Anna was careful to meet his eyes squarely before answering.

"Am I supposed to know what that is?"

She could feel the calculation in his gaze as he weighed her words, trying to distill truth from fiction. And in the seconds of silence that passed between them, Anna knew that whatever answer he found would determine how quickly she lived or died. She kept her wide eyes on him while trying to ignore the pounding in her head.

Just when she feared the tension in her body would betray her, he stepped back and resumed his seat, while opening up his little notebook again.

"A code talker is a person used by your government to translate war messages into obscure languages or codes that, so far, have been difficult for us to decipher. Our spies informed us that such a person had been moved to your base in Oahu recently. We need to find that person."

"Huh," Anna said casually. "Well I've never heard of anything like that."

"I see," Ichiro replied coolly. "And what type of work do you do in the Navy, Ms. Freeman? It is my understanding that there are not many Negro women who would be welcomed in such an environment."

"I'm a cook," she said evenly. "People have to eat, no matter what color they are."

"And are you a good cook, Ms. Freeman?"

Anna knew he was scrutinizing her every word. She needed to keep her story going, just like she'd practiced, but her headache was starting to blur her vision. She needed to lie down, but she didn't want to give him any reason to suspect her.

"Of course," Anna replied, with a dash of indignation that she hoped made her sound more convincing.

Ichiro looked at her doubtfully. Nothing about the woman sitting before him suggested domestication. Her hair, though slightly displaced from the attack and the journey, was twisted around her head in a perfect, u-shaped roll that would have been the envy of any Japanese starlet. Even though she was in obvious discomfort, her back was held straight from years of breeding and conditioning. He'd seen it before. And though he dare not touch her, her hands looked soft, with long, well-manicured fingers. He wasn't sure what this woman did, but only a fool would think that she spent any time slaving over a hot stove. And there was something else, too, in the tone of her voice. Her American accent was laced with something else that slipped in and out of her regular pattern of speech.

Why is she hiding? He wrote in his notebook before looking up to share his suspicions. But by the time he turned his attention back towards her, it was clear that her discomfort had grown into distress. Ichiro was up and at her side in an instant.

"Ms. Freeman, are you alright? Ms. Freeman, can you hear me?"

Anna heard him calling her name, but the sound was muted by the sharp ringing in her ears. The pain in her head seemed to heighten her senses, making everything suddenly too bright and too loud. She could feel the stiff threads of the bedsheets chaffing against the backs of her calves, and the taste of blood in her mouth was overwhelming as she bit her cheek to keep from trembling.

Still, determined to keep up her façade, she opened her mouth to respond only to fall backwards into his arms. There was a flash of light, then nothing.

"Ms. Freeman! Anna! Can you hear me?"

Ichiro tried to ignore the rush of adrenaline he felt as he checked her pulse, her eyes, her breathing. In his arms, she seemed to calm instantly, so that when he laid her back down on the bed, her gaze was soft and clear as she opened her eyes, looked up at him, and smiled. Confused, Ichiro touched her cheek, checking for fever, then froze as her hand crept up to hold his in place. A tear escaped her eyes as she closed them and let out a shuddering sigh. When she looked up at him again, her eyes were filled with open adoration.

"Ms. Freeman, are you alright? You seem to have had a . . ."

"Why do you call me by that name? Do you not know who I am, Ekow?"

Her voice was deep and rich, with an accent that was not there a few minutes ago. Ichiro stared at her in amazement, tingling with the caress of her hand over his and the strange sensation he felt in his chest every time she called him by that name.

"Do you not know my name, Ekow? Even in this form, I am not so unlike myself that you should not know me. I know you feel it, too. I can see it in your eyes. Will you not call me by my name, my love?"

Ichiro trembled before her as he began to understand. During his medical training, he'd read about the principles of split personality disorder, but he'd never had the opportunity to witness it firsthand. Logically, it appeared that this disorder would explain what she seemed to be experiencing, but it didn't explain how someone with such profound psychosis would've been allowed to serve on a military base. It also didn't explain how he knew her name.

She looked at him, patiently, expectantly. Her hold on his hand was gentle, but all-encompassing; he couldn't have moved away from her even if he wanted to. Trying to get a hold of himself, Ichiro decided to lie.

"I'm sorry, but I don't know . . ."

"Yes, you do. I know you do. Do not lie to me, Ekow, to satisfy this form you now inhabit. It is beneath you. It is beneath us both. Lie to the others if you must, but we are alone now, and if only for a moment, I have found you."

Ichiro leaned over, placing his other hand over her forehead so that to the men watching them behind the mirrored glass it might appear that he was examining her head wound. Softly, he whispered in her ear, "But we are not alone, Ama. In this place, we are never alone."

When Ichiro raised himself up again, he could see understanding creasing the lines of her face, but there was also relief and a clear joy that she tried hard to contain. With his back to the glass, he shielded her face from view as he inexplicably returned her smile.

"I knew you would come back to me," she mouthed before General Fukigama burst into the room.

"Does she have what we need?" the General demanded.

"This is highly improper. I'm conducting this investigation!" Ichiro replied.

"Yes, but it seems more like a reunion than an interrogation. Why does she call you by that name?"

"I believe the patient is suffering from split personality disorder. It is uncommon, but in London, I did hear of a few documented cases. I'd need more time to make a definitive assessment—"

"She is not your patient; she is our prisoner!" General Fukigama snapped. "We are not here to conduct tests, Commander. We are at war! We need answers. We need that code."

Ichiro had not realized he was holding Ama's hand until his commanding officer stepped between them and broke the connection.

"Who are you? What is your name?"

Ama sat up on the bed and narrowed her eyes. She looked at the stranger standing in front of her as if he was a dirty rag.

"My name is Ama, daughter of Kodwo, Chief of the Akumfi people. Who are you?"

"I am General Fukigama of the Imperial Navy. How did you come to be in the service of the Americans? Is your country allied with the US?"

"I don't know what you're talking about. I am ally to no one."

Frustrated, the General pressed on, "We intercepted a cable from the US to your base in Hawaii. We know they were sending a code talker to you. Do you have the code?"

Ama let out a husky, unconcerned laugh. "You have destroyed the barn, and now you look for the needle in the haystack? You are all fools! I do not know what you're talking about, and even if I did, I wouldn't tell you, nor will she. You are wasting your time."

"Who is 'she'? We have no other female prisoners here. What are you talking about?"

"I will say no more to you," Ama declared before turning away in defiance.

Ichiro stood back watching the exchange, trying to hide his reaction to Ama's words. From what little he knew about patients with split personality disorder, each personality was rarely aware of the other. But if she was aware of the difference between herself and Anna, what did that mean? Was his diagnosis wrong or was something else at play?

In a move that was meant to intimidate, the General stepped closer to Ama, but she refused to even meet his gaze. He noted with vexation that his proximity did nothing to ruffle her countenance, which remained confident and serene. The General was aware of only a few African nations that were aligned with the US, but none who would be stationed at a US Naval base. He would have to reconfirm his sources quickly if he was going to gain the leverage he needed.

"You will cooperate with us. One way or another," General Fukigama promised before turning abruptly and leaving the room.

Ichiro unclenched his fists along with the breath he'd been holding ever since the General had stepped closer to Ama. A part of him wondered how he would've survived attacking his CO in front of his entire base, but Ichiro also knew that the consequences would not have stopped him from protecting her if that had become necessary.

By the time he turned back to Ama, she had laid back down on the bed and was fast asleep.

※

Ichiro lay in bed that night unable to sleep. His quarters were only two buildings away from the medical facility, but he already felt too far. He could've easily slept in his office, but to do so would have aroused suspicion from the General and Private Sato that he couldn't afford, not if he was going to carry out his plans.

Tomorrow he would start again with Anna and try to ascertain first, if Anna was aware of this other presence and second, if she was, what did she know. Ichiro had already observed Private Sato questioning the prisoners under his charge and his best assessment was that all of them were lost causes, except for Lieut. James. From what Ichiro had observed, the other two men were too simple-minded to be entrusted with any sensitive information. Of course, Private Sato, in an attempt to make his part of the operation seem more important, had a different opinion. He thought that all three men could very well know critical information, and he wanted immediate permission to question them in any way he felt necessary to achieve results. Private Sato planned to observe their interaction a bit more before he decided whom to question first.

Sato's plans would not have concerned Ichiro except he knew that if he wasn't able to produce definitive results with Ms. Freeman, General Fukigama would turn her over to Private Sato, which was something Ichiro realized he would go to any lengths to avoid.

Though it disturbed him, Ichiro knew that it was a good thing that he and Ms. Freeman had been observed. If the others had not witnessed the obvious change in her personality for themselves, he knew they would not have believed him. But more than credibility, the incident bought him time—time to solve the mystery between what he knew and what he felt so that he could make sense of it for himself without interference.

"Tomorrow, I'll start again," he promised before drifting off into a restless sleep.

That night, he dreamt that he was walking in a vast plain filled with tall grass that rose to touch his fingertips. His limbs moved quickly in the darkness, and although Ichiro couldn't see where he was going, he was not lost. Tingling with anticipation, he began to run towards his destination. The night air was as exhilarating as the pull in his chest, driving him forward to close the distance between him and the woman waiting for him—the woman that he knew was Ama.

In the distance, Ichiro could see that she was standing at the edge of a cliff with her hair braided in two neat rows.

"Ama, wait for me!" he cried. As she turned to him, Ama reached out her hand, but she did not smile.

"Ekow," she whispered. "I am so sorry, my love." Alarmed by the sadness in her voice, he ran faster. There was no danger around that he could see, but her eyes told him that they were out of time.

"I'm coming!" he shouted, as tears began to run down her face.

"They cannot take me alive. Forgive me, Ekow," she whispered again, then stepped off the cliff and into the depths.

"Wait!" Ichiro screamed as he tumbled over the cliff after her. "Wait for me!" he cried as the mist swallowed them both.

Ichiro shot up in his bed, fighting the sheets that had wound themselves around his limbs. When he was calm and there was nothing left of the dream but a hollow ache in his chest, Ichiro got up from his bed and dressed for work. The morning would not come for several hours, but it didn't matter. He wouldn't rest, couldn't rest, until he saw her again.

If Ichiro had known that she would be awake, he would have knocked before entering. Throughout the small building that held their prisoners there was no sound. So, when he unlocked the door to Anna's room, he did not expect to disturb her. His only intention was to confirm that she was still alive. Instead, his intrusion was greeted with a sharp yelp of surprise.

"What are you doing here?!?"

The room was completely dark, so he didn't see her until he raised his lantern and found her pressed into the far corner of the room with a towel clutched to her bare chest. Immediately, he lowered the lantern and turned away.

"Get out!" she yelled.

"I'm sorry," Ichiro stammered. "I assumed you would be asleep. I just came to check on you." He could hear the sound of rustling behind him but he didn't dare turn around again.

The sincerity in his voice swept her suspicions away before she could pull them closer. Irritated at being disarmed so easily, Anna dressed quickly.

"If you thought I was asleep, why did you come?" she snapped. "And you can turn around now if you're staying."

Ichiro hesitated as his mind raced to come up with a good excuse. He took his time facing her, but when he did, he found her still in the corner fully dressed in the gray shirt and pants he'd left for her. Her thick hair was braided in two rows, which made her look younger than when he'd first seen her and even more like the woman in his dreams.

Lovely, he thought. The sight of her warm, alive and only a few feet away comforted him deeply.

"I wanted to make sure you had not used another one of your hairpins to try to escape again," he joked. "I'm just making my rounds, checking in on all the prisoners."

Anna shook her head and smiled, despite herself.

"And the others? Have they escaped?"

"None of them have hairpins," Ichiro replied. "So, I guess they decided to get a good night's sleep. You're the only one who's still awake. Why is that, Ms. Freeman?"

"I . . . couldn't sleep. When I woke up, I found the wash basin with warm water and soap, so I thought I would clean up a bit."

"I'm glad you found them useful."

"Did you do that?"

"I requested it, yes. I thought you would want to refresh yourself."

"Thank you," Anna replied cautiously. Everything about this man seemed cordial and trustworthy, which made him more dangerous. *You need to keep your guard up,* she reminded herself as she forced her attention away from how the lantern accentuated his strong beautiful features.

"You've been very hospitable, especially under the circumstances. I wonder if the male prisoners have been extended the same courtesies, or is there something you want from me in return?"

Even though Ichiro would never regret the sight of her smooth shoulders glowing in the light of his lantern, his motives couldn't have been farther from what she was insinuating.

"I assure you, Ms. Freeman, my only intention is to encourage your cooperation in answering my questions."

"Well, I can't help you. I don't know anything. Like I told you, I'm just the cook."

"Perhaps, but since you're up, I'd like to get a head start on another matter. One that is perhaps of less interest to my other colleagues."

"What other matter?"

"Please sit down." Ichiro backed away from her hospital bed in hopes of coaxing Anna from her corner of the wall.

When she did finally sit down, he opened the door and dragged in a chair from the hall before closing the door behind him. He took a seat, then opened up his small notebook.

"Are you comfortable, Ms. Freeman?" Anna nodded through a clenched jaw. "For the record, to whom am I speaking?"

"I told you my name already; you wrote it down in that book."

Ichiro nodded intently and leaned in, watching her face in the lantern carefully.

"Have you ever heard of a woman named Ama of the Akumfi tribe?"

This time Anna didn't have to feign confusion.

"I don't know who that is." As she spoke, an old, familiar shudder passed through her body, but she ignored it. It had been a long time since she'd felt it for the first time as a little girl. Over the years, she'd learned to dismiss it.

Ichiro scribbled something in his notebook, then shifted his attention back to Anna.

"I ask because you introduced yourself to General Fukigama as Ama yesterday."

"What? What is this?" Anna replied. "Is this some kind of joke? I don't know what you're talking about." Anna didn't feel nearly as defensive as she intended to sound. She was too confused for that. His line of questioning didn't make any sense, given what she knew his objectives should have been. Plus, the fact that he suggested that he wanted to keep their conversation private was also odd. Any information he got from her would surely be reported to his superiors, so what difference did it make? Of course, he could've been lying in order to gain her trust, but somehow she didn't think so. She decided to be honest for as long as it was in her interest to do so.

"So, you don't remember your exchange with General Fukigama, yesterday."

"No," Anna replied. "You're the only person I've seen since coming here."

Ichiro stared at her for a long time. There was no tension in her body as she spoke to him, only signs of genuine confusion and fear.

"What's the last thing you remember from our conversation yesterday?"

It had been a long time since Anna had heard that question. Not since "the spells" her parents told her she would have as a little girl. The pastor at her family's church had asked her about the voices she would make while playing by herself or talking with others. At first, Anna had not understood. She assured the pastor and her parents that the voice was her friend, who told the best stories about far-off places and parts of the world that no one knew about. Her parents became worried, and in response, Anna tried harder to explain and share the stories that the voice told her about, but the more she talked, the less her parents understood. Eventually, she stopped sharing the stories and asked her friend to go away, as the pastor had instructed, until slowly it did.

As an adult, whenever she thought back to that time, Anna dismissed it as a childhood fantasy—an imaginary friend for a lonely and slightly odd girl. She couldn't even remember the sound of her "friend's" voice, much less her name.

"I remember you asking me if I was a good cook. I remember telling you that I was."

Ichiro nodded. "Do you remember anything else?"

"I remember that my head began to hurt. There was a flash of light, I think. Then, I guess I fainted."

Ichiro wrote in his notebook.

"Has that ever happened to you before, to the best of your knowledge?"

"No," Anna lied, looking down at her hands. Her fear of becoming too comfortable with this man was rising. She needed to keep her distance, and discussing her childhood would not help her do that.

But even in the poorly lit room, Ichiro could see through her. He knew that she was lying, but what he didn't know was if it was to protect Ama or herself. He tried a different angle.

"Does the name Ekow mean anything to you?"

Again, the current ran through her body along with the sudden impulse to get up from her bed and fold herself into his arms, where she knew she would fit perfectly.

What the hell is happening? She asked herself as her hands dug into the sheets on either side of her body. She needed to turn the tables quickly before instinct took over and she did something rash.

"No," she said sharply, "Does that name mean anything to you?"

Ichiro had been expecting this retort. Her question was at the heart of why he was here before dawn talking with her.

Do not lie to me. It is beneath you. It is beneath us. She had said those words to him a few short hours ago. Even if Anna couldn't remember it, he would tell her the truth now.

"Yes, it does. It is the name you called me when we first captured you. You saw me and called out to me, 'Ekow, Ekow, upendo wangu.' It was the first thing you said."

Ichiro watched Anna's eyes widen in shock, then she looked away. Her reaction gave him an idea.

"Do you recognize the language? Do you know what it means?"

Of course she did. She knew the language and its translation, so she lied.

"I only speak English, Commander, and I have no idea why I would say . . . whatever it is I said to you."

"So you don't remember saying it, then."

"No."

Ichiro tucked his pencil inside his notebook and closed it. He could see that despite her best efforts to hide her hands, she was trembling. He leaned closer, then stood up. Any minute now, the day would begin. The facility would fill with soldiers, and he didn't know if they would ever get this chance again.

Slowly, he placed his hands on top of hers, so that his body leaned in and encased her on each side. He could feel the surge immediately, and as her eyes shot up to meet his, Ichiro knew she felt it, too.

"I'm afraid I don't believe you, Ms. Freeman. I don't speak whatever language it was you spoke to me that day, but I knew the name Ekow as soon as you said it, and as you fainted in my arms, I heard something —a word, Ms. Freeman and somehow I knew your name was Ama."

He could feel her hands trembling harder underneath his and held them tighter, hoping to push back her fear with the warmth he felt coursing through him.

"I don't know what this means or what is happening, but I know it means something and I believe you do as well. Whatever else you're hiding, Ms. Freeman, do not lie to yourself or me about this. You told me yesterday that it was beneath us and I believe you, even if you don't."

Ichiro held her gaze for as long as he could before finally stepping away. Just outside the door, he could hear the sounds of the day beginning. Someone was in the kitchen preparing food for the prisoners. Their time was up.

Ichiro left her sitting on her bed. He did not say goodbye, and it wouldn't have mattered even if he had. The energy between them seeped into her bones and lingered, no matter how hard she tried to make herself push it away.

Anna didn't see the Commander again that day, but she did eventually meet General Fukigama, who questioned her for hours. He too spoke of the woman she'd claimed to be when they first met and seemed quite perturbed when Anna insisted on having no knowledge of this other person.

"We will get the truth from you," he bellowed. "You will not play games with us!"

Anna found him so much easier to deal with than Commander Ichiro. His arrogance and rudeness were almost a comfort to her. She was trained for this. His insults and coarse tactics were almost comical. As a woman, a Black woman in the military, no less, belligerent attitudes were to be expected. She dealt with them in England throughout her studies and certainly at home, where women of any color were generally not considered of value to the US military effort. Her decision to join the war had been an unpopular one with her family, who had counted on Anna leveraging her college degree in mathematics to become a doctor or a teacher. When she decided to use her minor in languages to apply to the US Army's Women's Auxiliary Corp as a translator, everyone was shocked. When her application was denied due to restriction on Negro applicants, Anna applied and was accepted to Cambridge University's esteemed linguistics program, where she added four new languages to the three she already knew.

At first, the discrimination and isolation she experienced made her doubt her desire to join the war, but Anna knew that her parents had suffered far worse to provide a good life for her. They'd supported her aspirations even when they disagreed with them, and she was determined not to let their faith in her go to waste. Eventually, Anna's talent for translation and background in mathematics earned her an opportunity to train as a cryptologist, where she excelled. Anna's reputation and skill eventually led to her recruitment back to the US under a top-secret assignment.

Along the way, she had confronted many arrogant men. General Fukigama was just the latest. After exhausting himself in their interrogation, the General finally rose from his chair.

"We have ways, Ms. Freeman, to get you to talk. Do not think we will hesitate to use these tactics," he threatened.

"I'm sure you won't, General, but it won't matter," she said demurely. "I can't tell you anything you don't already know."

一つは、彼らがハウエルを呼び出す愚かなものに話よりも、ほとんど悪いです。

This one is almost worse than talking with that stupid one they call Howell, the General muttered to himself absently before turning his attention back to her.

To Anna, it looked like he wanted to strangle her, but his restraint held. Instead, without another word, the General got up from his chair and left the room, with his entourage of petty officers trailing quickly behind.

As soon as the door closed, Anna climbed into bed, exhausted from keeping up the façade of innocence for so long. Her shoulder ached. Her head was pounding, and she knew she needed to rest, because when he came back—and there was no doubt that General Fukigama would—she would have to choose between making him believe her or making him kill her in order to conceal the secret she held.

※

The next time Anna opened her eyes, she was not alone.

"What do these Japs want with us, anyway? Why are they holding us here?" Third Class Petty Officer Marvin Howell let out a terrible cough before continuing. The smoke from the fire had taken a toll on his lungs, but comparatively speaking, he was the least damaged of the bunch and therefore had the most energy to complain.

"Wish they'd just kill us and be done with it already."

Beside him, Lieutenant Colonel Malock James forced himself up onto his side, being careful not to move his lower body. His bed sheets were drenched with sweat. How long have I been asleep, he wondered as he reached out for the glass of water on the rusted metal stool beside his cot. Before he fell asleep, he'd been fairly sure that he had been there for about two days, but now he wasn't so sure. At least the water was cool and refreshing. He had the urge to press the glass to his face, but he didn't want to call attention to his weakness, so he sipped it casually, savoring every drop, then set the glass down as carefully as his shaking hands allowed before answering Officer Howell.

"I think they're looking for something or someone," he said. Lt. James was grateful that his voice came out clear and steady. There was no room for doubt among them, especially now. "They think we know what it is."

"Well, I don't know shit," Howell answered back, "and even if I did, I wouldn't tell them a damn thing!"

Second Petty Officer Louis Rice rolled over to face Howell, whose cot was jammed against the opposite wall to where he lay. "Everyone knows you don't know anything, you ignorant ass," he joked.

They all laughed for a second, trying to shake off the tension, until something occurred to Rice.

"Lieutenant, what makes you think they're looking for some—. Hey, wait a minute. Who the hell is that? They got some colored girl in here with us."

Despite the pain, Malock shifted purposefully in his bed so that he could see where Officer Rice was staring. For a second, no one said a word, until Howell broke the silence.

"What the hell is going on? How'd they get this nigger in here?"

It must have been the word that brought Anna awake and fully alert. In seconds, she'd moved from the concrete floor where she'd been sleeping to having her back pressed against the locked front door of their room. Moving so quickly made her head spin, and while she suspected her concussion had something to do with it, she could also taste whatever drugs they had given her at the back of her throat. With no memory of how she'd come to be here, Anna's eyes darted around the room, trying to clear her head enough to assess her surroundings.

I'm alone, she thought, the only woman in a room with three White men. From the smell that soured the air, she knew that at least one of them was badly injured. If she had to take a guess, she'd put her money on the man closest to her, the one who was sweating through his clothes. His brave face did little to disguise the pain and infection that were seizing his body. She felt sure she could kill him if she had to.

The one standing up was slightly shorter than she was and was staring at her with unrestrained malice. His emotions will get the better of him, she thought with some relief. She'd fought men like him before, men who despised and underestimated her at first glance. Anna knew how to use his arrogance against him. But she would need to watch the third man, at the opposite end of the room. He had no obvious wounds that she could determine from his upright position on the bed, but that was not what worried her. The man met her eyes without hesitation, assessing her openly as a woman and a threat. He's the most dangerous, she realized. He'll be watching my every move.

"You hear us talkin' to you, girl?" Howell barked. "Where da hell you come from?"

Despite her better judgment, Anna decided to try to reason with the man. Ignorance aside, these were Americans held captive on enemy territory, like her. She would do everything she could to help them.

"I was stationed with the USS Arizona as a cook. They captured me as I was on my way to duty."

"I ain't never seen no girl nigger in the Navy."

"You call me that again and you will never see anything else," Anna spat. She wanted to help, she really did, but if they were going to work together, she would have to set the ground rules—even if it meant leading the man before her out of here blind as a bat.

"Now hold on a minute! I ain't taking no sass from no ni—." Anna moved from the wall.

Lt. James forced himself into a fully upright position. "Shut up, Howell. Just shut the hell up! Okay, everybody just calm down!"

Even though he couldn't stand, Lt. James put his arms out between them, hoping it would stop Anna's advance. He didn't know who this woman was, but her eyes were sharp and focused. In a room full of men, he doubted that she was stupid enough to make a threat she couldn't follow through on.

"There're only four of us and God knows how many of them. We are Americans, for Christ's sake! If we're going to get out of here, then we've got to work together. So Howell, sit down and shut up. That's an order!"

Only when Howell had retreated to his cot did Anna settle herself back up against the wall.

"I'm Lt. Col. Malock James," he said firmly, "and that's P.O. Louis Rice and P.O. Marvin Howell. For better or worse, these are my men, and I promise you no harm will come to you by their hand. Why don't you start by telling us your name and how long you've been here."

While Anna appreciated Lt. James' sentiment, not a muscle in her back relaxed. He would be useless if any of them decided to attack.

"My name is Anna Freeman and I think I have been here for four days now, but I'm not exactly sure."

"Are there others here? Any Americans?"

"Not that I know of."

"Have they questioned you? Do you know what they want from us?"

Anna looked around the room cautiously. There were no mirrors, so she didn't believe they were being watched, but they were obviously put together for a reason. And just because they couldn't be seen didn't mean they couldn't be heard. If she lied, they would surely wonder why she was keeping secrets from her own countrymen.

"They have questioned me," she answered slowly. "They said something about a code talker. I told them that I didn't know what that was. Do you?"

Lt. James shook his head. He knew they were most likely being monitored and didn't want to give what little information he did have away. There had been rumors around the base, among a few high-ranking officials, that the Navy was sending them a code talker. From what he understood, the transfer was still in process, but he didn't have clearance for any details.

He tried to sit up a bit more, but his stomach felt nauseous. Sweat trickled down his neck and he feared that he would faint any minute. In an effort to shake it off, Lt. James threw the bed sheets back from his body. For a moment, the small breeze created by the motion was refreshing, but then he caught sight of his leg.

The stench was even more intense than the fear in Lt. James' eyes, but only Anna seemed to notice the smell as the others carried on unfazed. Lt. James could see that the bandage around the wound on his calf was black and greenish around the edges. Someone had left a small bottle of alcohol and clean gauze by his bed, but he'd been too afraid to see the full extent of his injury to dress the wound himself and too ashamed to ask one of the other men in the room to do it for him.

Anna stepped forward. "You need to clean that wound as soon as possible, before the infection gets any worse. I can help you. I know what to do."

"It's fine," James said, gritting his teeth. "I just need to eat something."

"You're probably too nauseated for that. I would stick to water until the infection is under control, if I were you," Anna blurted out before realizing that he was most likely trying to keep up a brave face for his men.

"How you know he got an infection?" Howell asked, sulking on his bed.

"Because I can smell it from clear across the room," Anna snapped, but she kept her eyes on James. By this time, Anna was almost near his bed. Lt. James looked up at her closely.

"Are you a nurse?" James asked. Malock had heard of colored doctors and nurses before. He'd even driven past a colored hospital once while he was visiting his aunt in Washington, DC, but he'd never met one before now. He didn't even know if there were any in the Navy, much less on the USS Arizona. A thought was beginning to come together in his mind, but with the fever, he couldn't hold it.

"Yeah," Rice chimed in. "How do you know so much about it?" Anna ignored him, choosing instead to focus on Lt. James' questions.

"No. I was studying to be a nurse before I signed up for the war, but they don't allow Negroes to serve as nurses, so I got assigned to the kitchen."

Anna knelt down beside him and added as quietly as she could, "The wound is beginning to fester. It needs to be irrigated and cleaned. I can help you, but it's going to hurt. You have to be certain that you can keep quiet."

There it is again, he thought. The slight inflection in her speech. Hearing it again, so close to him, he was surer than before—British. It was definitely British. Somehow she had spent some time there, enough to pick up an accent. How does that happen to an American colored woman? he wondered, trying to put the pieces of her together. He was about to ask her when the pain surged again in his leg and he realized he had more pressing things to worry about.

Refocusing his attention, James looked at Anna with hardened eyes, searching hers for any trace of doubt that she could do what she claimed. He knew gangrene was beginning to set in, and if he had a chance of saving his leg, he needed to act as soon as possible.

"Give me a pillow," was all he said in response, but Anna knew she had his trust and his permission.

"And can someone get me some water, preferably some you haven't drunk from already?" Anna asked. When she didn't get a response, she looked around the room. It was clear that none of the men were willing to help her, so she got up from the floor and grabbed the water pitcher from the front of the room.

"You're just a regular Florence Nightingale, aren't you, girl?" Rice quipped. "I wonder what other talents you got." His voice dripped with suspicion, but she couldn't waste time dealing with him now.

Not knowing how much time they had before their captors decided to show up, Anna worked quickly, handing Lt. James the pillow only a moment before she unwrapped the bandage from his leg. She knew the pain must have been excruciating, but while he trembled violently, he never made a sound. When half the alcohol was used and the new bandages were almost in place, Anna leaned back and touched his arm gently while reaching for what was left of the gauze.

"It's done," she said softly. "I don't know if we can stop the infection, but if you change the bandages regularly, you might have a chance. I can do it for you if you like."

"I wouldn't let no nigger nurse wait on me," Howell mumbled under his breath, but just loud enough for Anna to hear him.

"Shut up, you cretin! No wonder the General thinks you're an idiot!"

She realized her mistake immediately.

Beside her, Lt. James squeezed her arm tightly. When she turned to him, Anna could see the warning in his eyes as he shook his head, but by that time, it was already too late.

"How do you know what they say about Howell? They never speak anything but Japanese around us." A sudden pain in his side forced Rice to adjust his body, exposing the bandages that were wrapped tightly around his lower torso. "Dressing a wound better than any doctor I've ever seen, speaking Japanese – you sure know a whole lot for a cook."

Anna could feel his cold eyes boring down on her, before she turned to face him with a sarcastic smirk.

"Speak Japanese? Please!" Anna replied with a tense laugh. "They told me about Howell in English and now that I've met him, I see why. You don't need to speak Japanese to know he's a fool."

She hoped it worked. She hoped it would be enough, but by the look in Rice's eyes, she knew it wasn't.

"Well, I'll be damned" Rice began, as if seeing her truly for the first time.

"What? What y'all sayin? That this . . . she the one they . . ."

Lt. James turned to Howell. "Not another word out of your mouth, Howell!" he hissed. "Not one goddamn word. You hear me?"

Howell and Rice fell silent, as Anna turned her attention back to the Lieutenant. Her voice was slightly shaken, but clear.

"Like I was saying, the bandages—"

The door to the small room flew open before she could finish.

"What is this?" Private Sato demanded, stepping between Anna and the Lieutenant. At the abrupt intrusion, Anna lost her balance and fell to the ground.

"Which one of you is hiding the code talker? Tell us now!"

No one uttered a word.

Turning to his guards, Private Sato roared. "Pick one, any one! The General is growing impatient. We need answers!"

The two officers that came in with Private Sato looked around the room, then zeroed in on Petty Officer Howell.

Fear gripped her heart as she watch them pick Howell up and drag him across the floor kicking and screaming. While his screams might have been incoherent to non-native speakers, Anna understood him perfectly. "Not me! Not me!" he shouted. "I'm not the one you want!"

Rice and James looked at Anna, one with cautious malice in his eyes, and one with growing resolve. Lt. James forced himself upright on the bed.

"Take me!" he yelled, reaching out for Private Sato's arm. "Take me and I'll tell you everything I know."

Anna's heart fell as she watched Lt. James attempt to stand before collapsing on top of her on the floor. It was only a moment before they lifted him up and turned Lt. James towards Private Sato's satisfied sneer, but he only needed a second to convey his message. "No matter what, keep the code," he whispered into her ear.

As they dragged him from the room, she never got a chance to say thank you or goodbye.

Silence hung in the vacuum created by Lt. James' absence, but Anna could feel their eyes on her and prepared herself for whatever anger and blame they might throw her away.

"Is it worth what he gave," Rice whispered, "to keep whatever secret you know?" The bitterness in his voice was tempered by a sobering fear. "If I'm gonna have to do that, I need to know it's worth it."

Sitting up on the floor, Anna quieted her own grief enough to look Officer Rice in the eye.

"It is," she said simply.

Rice nodded, while Howell scoffed.

"I don't care what you know. I ain't dying on account of one, lying, dirty ni—."

The door flew open again, just as Anna was getting to her feet to finally make good on her promise. Private Sato stormed back into the room with two more men, each with their fingers on the trigger of a gun.

"Which one of you bandaged the prisoner's leg?"

With guns in their faces, Rice and Howell were too stunned to say a word, but their eyes fell straight to Anna.

"I did," Anna admitted, standing between Private Sato's men and Rice and Howell.

"Take her!" Sato ordered just before a black sack was thrown over her head and she was shoved from the room.

In moments she was thrown against a hard surface.

"I thought you were a cook! Who taught you to clean wounds?" Private Sato demanded.

"I was a nurse before," Anna stammered, trying to move as far away from him as she could with the bag still over her head.

"His wounds were not meant to heal," Private Sato hissed before slamming the door behind him and locking her inside.

Then who brought the alcohol and bandages, Anna almost asked aloud just before the answer occurred to her—Commander Oimikado. Ichiro is probably the only one in this place who would have had the kindness to do it, she thought, with a strange sense of pride.

Removing the black bag from her head proved needless. There was no light to see anything in the place they kept her, but she was fairly sure she'd never been in this room before. The space was significantly smaller than the medical ward where she'd first woken up as well as the holding cell where she met Lt. James. And though the walls of the small room felt like concrete, they must've been paper thin, because she could hear every sound Lt. James made as they tortured him.

It went on for hours, but he never uttered her name. He never gave her up. But Anna knew that torturing him was only part of their plan. They wanted to torture her as well. That was the reason she was placed in a room so close to his, so she could hear his fate while having ample time to contemplate her own.

And it worked. As the drugs they gave her wore off and exhaustion took over, Anna cried with Lt. James as he screamed out in pain, often into her own hands so their tormentors could not hear. Then, when his silence stretched on long enough that she knew he was dead, Anna cried again and thanked God for His mercy.

Every nerve in her body ached with the strain of hearing his torture and being unable to do anything about it. But she still had the presence of mind to wipe her tears as light from the fixture above suddenly flooded her room and the door opened.

Her eyes hurt from the prolonged darkness, so it took her a moment to look up and see Private Sato's satisfied expression.

"I apologize for keeping you waiting. Questioning Lt. James took a bit longer than I expected."

Anna could taste the adrenaline as it flooded her mouth. In all her years, she'd never been so close to death. She knew that taking Sato's life would most certainly seal her own fate, but she didn't care. If she could make him pay dearly for the agony Lt. James had suffered, it would be more than worth the price. But when Anna went to move she found she couldn't. There was a sudden sharp pain in her temple and a flash of light between her eyes. When she went to speak, she didn't recognize the voice as her own.

"Do you believe in heaven, Private Sato?"

Momentarily taken aback, Private Sato narrowed his eyes. "Only death is certain," he replied.

"Indeed, for you and for me, but your death will be unprecedented in its horror, as merciless as you have been today."

"If I were you, I would be more concerned about my own death," he said. "You must have heard Lt. James' screams. It has clearly affected you."

"As anyone should be when faced with such cruelty."

"Cruelty?" he said, stepping forward. "Like starving innocent children? How dare you speak to me of cruelty! What have you suffered? I do what I do for my country!"

Ama could not argue with the truth of his words, but it did not change the outcome.

"Nonetheless, you will lose this war."

"Not before I get what I need from you."

Ama stepped back. "Where is Commander Oimikado? I will only speak with him."

Private Sato laughed.

"Do you think he will save you? What is it between you two?"

When Ama didn't answer, he continued. "He's not even here. General Fukigama and his favorite officer went to a private meeting, leaving me in charge today! Unlike Commander Oimikado, I intend to have results for the General when he returns."

The drugs, her move to the men's cell, and Lt. James' torture—suddenly, the events of the day began to make sense.

"When Commander Oimikado returns, you will be punished for what you have done."

"Not if it proves effective," Private Sato replied confidently. "But I think I understand your obsession now. You're in love with him, aren't you?"

When Ama's face set in indignation, Private Sato shook his head and laughed. "Oimikado said you were crazy, but I didn't believe him until now. You would have to be to fall in love with your enemy and a married man. I wouldn't get my hopes up if I were you."

Ama blinked, stunned. "What do you mean, married? That's not possible."

"I assure you, it is. He is promised to some rich girl from Tokyo. I can't remember her name now, but believe me when I tell you that they would have been married already if he had not signed up for the war."

The stricken look on Ama's face made it too hard for Private Sato to resist continuing to taunt her. "I hear she's quite beautiful. A proper Japanese lady."

Ama's dismay turned quickly to rage.

"Liar!" she roared as she lunged forward and slapped him hard across the face. "He belongs to me!"

Private Sato fell back in shock from the sheer power of the blow. He would not have expected a woman of her size to be capable of delivering such force. His hand reached up to soothe his stinging cheek and returned with three crimson lines across his palm.

She hadn't even noticed that her own fingernails were curled at her side and coated with blood.

His hands were around her neck in an instant, and though Ama clawed and fought with all her might, she was no match for the vice-like grip in which he held her.

"Insolent wretch!" he hissed as he drew closer and tightened his fingers around her throat. Ama could feel consciousness slipping away, and she dug her nails deep into his wrists as if holding on to her own life.

But the more she held on, the less she was able to breathe until she could feel her own death closing in.

Not yet. I can't leave him, she thought in horror, just before Private Sato's grip was suddenly gone. His body crumpled before her as she fell to her knees. Gasping for breath, Ama slumped down to the floor. She could hear Sato's limp body being dragged away, but with her eyes closed, she did not see the one who had saved her sit down beside her on the floor and touch her gently on the shoulder. Nor did she care to.

"I'm sorry," Ichiro began, "I am so sorry I was not here. I tried to get back as soon as I could. How badly did he hurt you?" I will make him pay for ever thinking he could touch you, Ichiro added silently.

Ama had always known that he would come. All she needed was to give him time to get to her. Her only intention had been to hold on long enough to find out the truth.

"Is it true . . . ?" she asked, despite the pain it caused her to speak.

Ichiro froze beside her, unsure of what to say.

After a moment, Ama straightened slightly, but kept her eyes closed. She couldn't bear to look at him, to see in his eyes what he would not say.

"Is it true that you are promised to another?"

Ichiro's mouth hung open in confusion. Who is she now? Is this Anna or Ama? he wondered, before remembering the soft foreign accent in her voice. Still, he wanted, needed, to be sure.

Shifting his body so that he could see her face clearly, he realized that she was trembling. From the shock of the attack or something else, he did not know. Her eyes were closed to him in defiance, until he reached out, despite himself, to touch her face. The intense emotion that coursed through him every time he touched her was mirrored on her face as her eyes opened to meet his. A familiar softness. A familiar touch. And he knew. This was Ama.

"Is it true?" she asked a third time with the evidence of so much pain brimming in her eyes.

Thinking of his intended, Naoko, it didn't seem possible that he even knew her. His whole life, everything before the last few days seemed so far away from the reality of this woman before him. How could he be betrothed to someone else? In the face of Ama, this woman he didn't even know, the whole arrangement with Naoko didn't seem real. All day, while he was away, Ichiro tried to re-ground himself in the realities he knew, but none of them compared to the gravity of her.

"I'm sorry," he stammered, "I don't—"

"What do you not know?" Ama shouted. "How could you not know to wait for me as I have waited for you? Lifetimes, Ekow!" She paused for a moment, her voice breaking on his name, the name she called him that was not his. "I have suffered lifetimes to find you! How could you not know that you belong to me?"

The tears were spilling from her eyes, but the anger was gone, replaced with a certainty that he had not seen and did not know was true until he looked at her.

The answer Ichiro wanted to give—that he did not know her and he was not who she believed him to be—felt profoundly false, but he also could not give her a truth he did not have. He could only stare back at her in a silence that seemed to replace her certainty with despair.

Slowly she leaned into him, resting her head on his neck in a way that was so intimate, as if they had done it a thousand times before, except he had never been like this with anyone. As she lay there motionless, then asleep in his arms, he couldn't stop thinking of the look in her eyes, the certainty that seemed to overwhelm any logic he might suggest.

Weaving his fingertips through the thick edges of her hair, Ichiro sat for a long time before finally answering her question with the impossible truth that was rising up from somewhere inside him.

"I did not know you were coming, Ama," he said to her more softly than a whisper. "I did not know."

When Anna opened her eyes again, she was back in the medical room where she'd started. Beside her, Ichiro lay asleep in a chair. With his eyes closed from the reality of who and what they were, he looked younger than he normally appeared. Innocent, Anna thought, and wondered if the same was true of her, that in dreams we're all innocent of the crimes we commit.

Anna stared at Ichiro, savoring the quiet moment between them as she remembered her exchange with Private Sato, how she'd been willing and ready to attack him until something else inside her took hold. She was not nearly as afraid as she thought she would be at the resurgence of her long-lost imaginary friend.

Two separate consciousnesses residing in one body. Well, how about that! I wasn't a troubled little girl after all, Anna thought. I'm just a totally insane adult.

Whatever the diagnosis, Anna knew it didn't matter. The unexplainable connection between them was real. The man sleeping in front of her was important in ways she was only just beginning to understand. And as Anna opened her mind again and listened like she'd done when she was a child, Ama told her about who the man before her had been, about the heartbreak of the first time they were torn apart, and the endless cycle of life that seemed to bring them back to each other again and again.

And when Ama was finished, they lay together in the silence of memory and cried for everything that would never be and the fact that destiny seemed to be conspiring against them once more.

Anna had not realized that she'd fallen asleep until the screams of Officer Howell woke her up.

"You bastards! You goddamn bastards!" he cried.

The sound of her own heartbeat pounded in her ears as she jumped out of bed. It was dark and she was alone.

What time is it? How long have I been asleep?

Where is Ichiro?

The moment she thought his name, he appeared in the doorway. His face looked tired and drawn.

"What's happened?" she asked.

"The General has consented to Private Sato's methods. Officer Rice was taken and died of his injuries early on this evening. A . . . message was just delivered to Officer Howell."

Anna's eyes widened in terror. "Oh my God."

"His reaction is . . . understandable," Ichiro whispered. The shame colored his neck and face, and he would not meet her gaze until she walked right up to him.

"How long have I been asleep?"

"A little less than 24 hours. I almost woke you, but you looked so peaceful that I didn't want to disturb you until there was no other choice."

"Ichiro, you have to help me. I need to get out of here."

Ichiro stared down at her as if in a daze. From this close, she could see the deep circles under his eyes.

"They will not harm you. I would never allow it, and the General would never allow a woman to be treated so . . ."

Anna turned from him in desperation. How could she tell him that it was not her own torture she was worried about? If that was all, there would hardly be anything to fear. How could she tell him that it was what they might gain, what she might say in delirium or utter unknowingly that she feared most? With only Officer Howell left to question, she had no doubt that they would discover who she was before long.

"When will they take Officer Howell?" she asked with her back still turned away.

"In the morning, but . . ." Ichiro walked around to face her. "The others gave us nothing, Anna. They swore they didn't know anything, even at the end. Why are you concerned about Officer Howell?"

Anna kept her eyes trained on the wall behind him.

"Anna, what does he know?"

"I need your help," she said finally.

Ichiro backed away, shaking his head. "I'm an officer in the Imperial Navy. What you're asking me to do goes beyond my connection to you. What you're asking me to do is treason."

"You're an intelligent man, Ichiro. You can't condone what the Third Reich stands for."

"I don't, but I can't let my own people starve while I do nothing. My duty is here."

"I understand that. I do, but this is bigger than our two countries. The world we know cannot survive if Germany wins this war. I don't care what alliance Japan has, life as we know it will be destroyed if Germany wins."

Ichiro turned to her with conflict raging in his eyes. "We are talking about my home, my country. You can't ask me to just . . ."

Anna closed her eyes then and let Ama speak the things even she could not say.

"There is no your people or my people, Ekow. There are just people. In this whole ugly world, there is just you and me."

Ichiro shook his head. "That can't be true," he said, heading towards the door. "It can't be," he said again, then left. Ama watched as he walked away, shoulders weighed down by all his burdens. With a sadness that broke her heart, she could see the man her beloved had become. Though the chains he wore now were invisible, just like before, there was no way that she could free him.

"But it is true," she whispered back. "It is," she said again, already preparing herself for what Anna planned to do.

※

With her shoulder still not fully healed, it took a while for Anna to tear bed sheets apart and weave them into something strong enough to support her weight. The military had trained her in every possible way to take her own life. It was a necessary skill, the one rule every code talker had to abide by—never to be taken alive. If she'd had a choice, she would have preferred another way—knife, injection, anything but hanging. But she didn't have a choice. Her medical room was meticulously free of quick and easy suicide options. So she resolved to make do with what she had.

Still, the work took her mind off what was to come. Regret stuck in her throat as she thought about all the people she would never get to say goodbye to and all the places she would never get to see, things she would never get to do. Inside her, Ama wept for how far she had come to gain so little, and how it would hurt him when he found her body and realized his mistake.

But Anna pressed on, winding her makeshift rope over an exposed pipe in the ceiling. She only had hours, if that, until Howell was dragged from his cell. Anna doubted that he would even make it out of the room before giving her up. When she was recruited back to the US, Anna had so many hopes and dreams for herself, her family, and a life filled with possibilities. The irony that she would kill herself using the same method so many of her race spent their lives trying to escape back home was not lost on her.

I need to do this now before I lose my nerve, she told herself while pulling the bed in place.

As she climbed up and slipped her head through the noose, Anna wondered what they would tell her mother, but then with a smile she realized that in all likelihood, she'd been reported among the dead at Pearl Harbor already and her family would be spared any knowledge of this.

"God forgive me," she prayed as she tightened the rope around her neck and prepared to step off the bed.

"Maybe He will, but I won't."

At the sound of his voice, Anna whirled around, almost losing her balance on the bed before loosening the noose, jumping down and running into Ichiro's arms. For a moment, she simply stood there, shaking in the safety of his crushing embrace.

"I didn't think you would come back."

"I'm sorry you ever had room to doubt it."

"I never thought I would have to . . ."

"And you won't again, not without me."

Anna could only hold him closer in response. Closing her eyes to the sound of his beating heart, she could feel the tension in their bodies seep away. It struck her then, that in some lifetime long ago, this ritual of just being near him had always calmed her.

"Anna, look at me," he whispered from above her. "Before we do this, I need to ask you something."

She lifted her face to his and saw the anguish in his eyes. "Do you know who I am?"

Anna forced herself not to look away, not to hide the vulnerability that had always been considered a weakness by the strong men in her life. But looking into his eyes, she knew that would never be true with this man. With this man, her greatest strength would always lie in being herself. And so she let the tears fall for him to see as the strange certainty of them filled her.

"Yes. I don't know how or why, but I know who you are, who we are, who we have always been."

His large hands came up to envelop her small face, wiping the tears away with his thumbs.

"Then we are the same, Anna. We are the same." Tears mingled with the joy in their eyes as they stood together once more.

Ichiro hated to break the small peace they had only just found, but it was necessary.

"Anna, we have to go. Here, put this on," he said, reaching into the satchel on his hip to hand her a thick overcoat.

"Where are we going?" she asked while buttoning the coat hastily.

"Into the mountains. It's a long, steep climb to the caves, but the mist should keep us out of sight once we reach the foothills. Are you ready?"

Anna nodded then took the hand he extended towards her. This time, there was no hesitation. With fingers clasped together, they closed the door behind the place that had been her prison and crept into the night.

By the time they heard the sirens, Anna and Ichiro were already at the foothills. Climbing was treacherous with no light to guide them. The mist covered everything ahead and behind, but Ichiro knew these mountains well having climbed them as a boy, so even though he could not see clearly, he still had a good sense of where they were going.

Determined to get as far as they could, they climbed all through the day light, stopping only to eat small bites of the salted fish and rice that Ichiro had packed for them. They didn't talk much, but there was no awkwardness between them. For the first time since meeting each other, they were alone, and at least for the night, there would be time.

When they reached the place that Ichiro spoke of, the mist had gone from white to gray with the setting sun. Anna gasped in amazement as they walked into a cave that seemed to go deeper and deeper into the heart of the mountain.

"Careful," Ichiro whispered as they walked down a steep set of stairs. "The rock is slippery here." He held her hand firmly as he navigated down until they reached an opening. Once the ground was flat, Ichiro lit a candle and held it out to her so that she could explore. The black stone of the cave around them sparkled with flecks of pale granite that shimmered like diamonds.

"It's like a cover of stars," she said while tracing the twinkling with her fingers.

"I'm glad you like it," he whispered from directly behind her.

Anna turned around to face him. "How did you know this place was here?"

"This was my secret place as a child. Back then, I could make it up here in half the time and still be home before my mother would miss me. There's even a hot spring over there."

Anna stepped away to see the small oval-shaped basin for herself.

"I brought some soap. I thought you might like a bath . . ."

His voice trailed off as he watched her trace the carving he made on the wall as a boy.

"Ichiro The Great," she chuckled, translating his words easily.

"I knew you could speak Japanese," he said with a grin.

"I speak a lot of languages. Eight in all, including English."

"I only speak two," Ichiro replied a bit sheepishly.

Anna's smile was warm as she came closer. "Luckily, they're the only two we need."

She stopped in front of Ichiro as he was taking off his jacket.

"Do we have a change of clothes?"

Ichiro hesitated. "I brought two night shirts. That's all I could fit into the bag." He reached down and pulled them out of his satchel.

"They're perfect. Thank you," she smiled, taking off her coat. "Now, we can lay these out to dry while we sleep."

"Yes," Ichiro murmured. Stepping closer, he savored the bow of her full mouth curling upwards as she watched him watch her undress.

"The way you look at me," she whispered. "It feels so familiar and yet . . ."

When she got to the top button of her shirt, he stilled her hands.

"May I?" he asked softly. Anna paused. It was hard not to give into the pull of those big, brown eyes. "Looking at you feels natural, as if I've been doing it every day of my life."

Anna moved in, wanting to be closer.

"And what would you do if you had seen me every day?"

"I would kiss you and undress you and never let you go."

"Then do it," Anna whispered.

He didn't hesitate, grabbing her to him with a force that matched his gaze. Though his grip was firm, his kiss was soft and caressing as his lips melted into hers, igniting something they both had never experienced before. Their lips moved together perfectly, leaning and pressing, equal parts longing and fulfillment. Ichiro moaned into her as she opened her mouth to let him in and the tighter he held her, the closer she felt to being free.

Afterwards, they pulled apart gasping for air, as their hands reached for places they both had only dreamt of touching. Anna ran her hands down the length of his nose and over his strong jaw as Ichiro traced the sensuous curves of her lips with his own, over and over again.

"You are everything to me now, Anna. Everything," he whispered.

Tears pricked her eyes and closed her throat as she leaned up to kiss him again.

"I know. And you are mine," she replied breathlessly. "You belong to me."

After undressing and stepping into the pool, they bathed each other in between kisses that fell as soft and slow as the water that ran over their bodies. And when they were done, they made love by the light of a single candle in the water that washed them clean and made them whole again. Reverence gave way to desire and the need to erase all the lifetimes that had kept them apart and in the safety of Ichiro's cave they became once more what they had always been.

Afterwards, as they lay spent on the floor of the cave under a single blanket, Ichiro tried to push away the thought of what might have happened if he failed.

"I was afraid I wouldn't reach you in time," he whispered into Anna's neck as he pulled her closer.

"But you did reach me," Anna reassured him, kissing the fingers of his hand. "You did," she said again before drifting off to sleep in his arms. Lying together they were warm and content until morning. By the time Ichiro woke, almost half the morning had already passed without them realizing it.

Ichiro moved quickly around the cave, dressing and eating his share of the rations while watching her sleep. It was, he thought, in all his years and all his wandering, the happiest moment of his life. To let it linger was foolish, and yet to disturb it would've been more so. Sometime during the night, Ichiro had loosened her braids, wanting to sink his fingers into the thick coils of her hair, which now crowned her head in a tumultuous cloud that made his fingers itch to touch them again, but discipline made him look at his watch.

It's 8:42am already, he sighed.

He knew Anna was strong and could move quickly if they needed to, but if they had any chance of maintaining the distance between them and the small army General Fukigama would surely have sent after them, they needed to leave now.

Slowly, he crept toward where Anna had rolled onto her back and lowered himself on top of her. Even with her eyes closed, her arms reached out to embrace him. He couldn't help, but smile.

"アンナは、我々が残しています。、甘いものを覚まします。目を覚ます。"

Anna, we have to leave. Wake up, sweet thing. Wake up.

"知っている。" *I know*, she mumbled.

"What time is it?"

"It's late," he said, kissing her lips. "You need to eat, then we have to go."

"Can I dress before we go?" she teased, wriggling playfully under the weight of his body.

Ichiro paused as if giving the question deep consideration. "No," he said finally.

"Is that so?" Anna replied, narrowing her eyes. Ichiro nodded defiantly.

"Ok." In an instant, Ichiro was on his back as Anna toppled him, planting a lingering kiss before rising and letting the blanket fall from her body. Ichiro drank in every move she made with pleasure.

It took them less than ten minutes to eat, dress, pack and leave the cave. They stepped out of the cave opening that had seemed so dark and mysterious yesterday into the bright mid-morning sun. There was not a drop of mist nor a cloud in the sky.

"Oh no," Anna said in dismay. Looking around her, every path was illuminated, every rock as clear as day. Whatever advantage they gained last night was surely lost.

"How close?" she whispered.

Ichiro's face was grave as she turned to him. All the happiness she had seen a few minutes ago was gone. He grabbed her hand and pulled her forward.

They climbed at twice the pace they had the day before. The wind cut through their clothes as they moved higher and higher up the mountain, but they did not stop until the sun set and a light snow began to fall. All day, the altitude had challenged them as the air got colder and thinner, but while they were moving, they were too focused to let it slow their progression. But as the sun's warmth waned, the reality of fatigue and a night without the shelter of their star-lit cave set in.

The best they could find was a small ledge that the wind had carved from the side of the mountain. Anna spread the blanket out for Ichiro to join her as they settled in against the rock that would shield them from the worst of the storm.

Passing the water bottle between them, Anna smiled.

"You know, they trained me for this at a small military base in Buffalo, NY. We had to sleep in the snow. When I found out that I was going to be stationed in Hawaii, I didn't think I'd ever get a chance to use my training, but now look. As my mother always says, 'nothing is ever wasted.'"

Ichiro looked down at her, surprised by her good mood despite the circumstances.

"And what do you think your mother would say about this?" he asked, pulling her closer so that her head was tucked securely under his chin.

"Believe it or not, she'd probably be happy."

"I can't imagine that," he chuckled while offering Anna the last of their water. After finishing the bottle, Anna leaned out to place his bottle next to hers, just outside the crevice, where they could catch the falling snow.

Anna laughed as she curled back into him. "No. I'm serious. All she's ever wanted was for me to quit all this military nonsense and settle down with a good man."

"Well, then I'm glad to have made her wish come true," Ichiro replied. He kissed the top of her head before adding, "Tomorrow we'll start at first light, make our way down the other side of the mountain. From there, we'll hire a boat to one of the other islands—doesn't matter which—and we'll figure out what to do from there."

In response, Anna kissed his chest, locking her arms around him tightly, but said nothing, and as the minutes ticked on, Ichiro knew.

"Anna, what is it? Tell me."

Anna shifted her body so that she could see his face as she spoke.

"You know, I never thought I would find a man that I could love before you. I've always thought that men liked women who follow, and I never wanted to follow anyone . . . Or, they liked women who could lead them, and I've never wanted to lead a man. I just wanted someone who would walk with me and be with me and somehow we would be walking in the same direction, and now here you are . . ."

"I am here, Anna."

"I know and I want you to know that I love you. The person I was and the person I am loves you, but no matter how far we get, no matter what happens, they can't take me alive. Do you understand? I can't risk it."

Ichiro looked at her for a long time. From the first time he spoke to Anna, he realized that he'd known that she was the code talker. But now, looking into her eyes, he finally understood the burden she carried, the weight of everything at stake if she failed to keep what was given to her. He would have to carry it, too.

"I promise." he said, kissing her solemnly. "I promise."

Ichiro stayed awake long after Anna had fallen asleep, afraid of closing his eyes, but eventually, he did.

Ama came to him naked, except for a small strip of cloth that she wore low on her hips and a necklace of seashells that he had given her that she never took off. Her skin shone like roasted coffee beans in the sun. It made him burn to touch her, to feel the warmth of her skin, but the Visiting ceremony had barely begun and they wouldn't be alone again for hours.

"Patience," his mother teased. Leaning in closer, she whispered, "Soon, Ichiro. Wake up! They are here!"

Ichiro startled awake to find his arms empty.

"Anna!" he shouted. "Anna, where are you?"

She came running from the other side of the ridge.

"I'm here. I'm here! I didn't mean to frighten you. I just didn't want to wake you."

Ichiro felt the air rush back into his lungs as she closed the distance between them.

"Baby, are you ok? You look so . . ."

"Yes. I'm all right. I was just worried."

"I know we have to go, but just for a second, come look at this. It's so beautiful."

Ichiro followed her to the other side of the ridge with eyes that would not stop filling with tears. As soon as they reached the other side, she let go of his hand, walking towards the edge of the cliff as the first light of day shone over the water. Everything around them—from the snow on the ground to the surface of the water—was bathed in pure pink light. When she reached the edge, Anna turned back to him, smiling.

She looks so childlike, he thought, so innocent with her hand extended out to me.

"Come see," she beckoned.

That's when Ichiro noticed that her hair was braided again in two rows. Her smile slipped and faded as they both heard the voices from behind.

"音はここから来ました。私は彼を聞きました！私は彼が彼女の名前を呼ぶのを聞きました！" *The sound came from here. I heard him! I heard him call her name!*

They froze as understanding passed between them. They had left Ichiro's blanket with their only weapons and supplies tucked into the other side of the ridge, which would soon be crawling with the General's men.

"彼らはここにいます！私は、毛布を袋を参照してください。" *They're here! I see a bag, blankets,* one man said.

"彼らは接近していなければなりません。それらをチェック！すべてをチェック！彼らは、これまで行っていることはできません！" *They must be close. Check them! Check everything! They can't have gone far.*

Ichiro stepped beside Anna and took her hand.

"Isn't it beautiful, Ichiro?" Anna said, as her tears made prisms with the light.

"It is. I'm glad you woke me up so that we could see it together."

"I love you," she whispered. Her voice broke over the very sight of him beside her, tall and magnificent against the rising sun.

"As I love you," Ichiro replied.

"How do we . . . ?" Anna's voice barely made a sound, but he understood exactly what she could not say.

Ichiro smiled through his tears. "Walk with me, love. Walk with me now."

From behind them, someone yelled, "それらを停止！" *Stop them!*

They turned then, to look out on the horizon as the first rays of true sun burst forth, and in its dazzling light, Anna and Ichiro stepped out into their future.

Part IV

After Today
April, 2051 ~ *The State of the District of Columbia, Washington*

*I*N MY OPINION, some things should stay old school. I remember looking at my parents' wedding pictures back when I was a kid. Everyone was present. There was a real ring that my father placed on my mother's hand, and the cake was made of flour, sugar and vanilla extract, rather than neural impulses fed selectively to the brain. Call me old-fashioned, but I think that's the way it's supposed to be.

Nowadays the hot trend with my crowd, the soon-to-be-thirties, is virtual weddings. For a few thousand credits, you can head into your nearest Simulation, or "Sim" Center, and rent your own wedding simulation "party pod" where you and all your guests can eat cake made up of figments of someone else's imagination. Though the wedding party typically still gets together in person, other guests can simply "plug-in" to the wedding from any place in the world that has a compatible simulation pod. I understand it makes weddings cheaper than they used to be, but I don't know if it's worth it. It just seems wrong to me to start something real in a place that doesn't exist.

My mother says I was born old, but I'm cool with that. Throughout grade school and college, my books and my demeanor have saved me from all manner of foolishness. My parents didn't have much, but what they did have, they spent on my education. Gratitude and the responsibility of making good on their investment in my dreams taught me discipline and focus. Which is how, after a long night of bachelor partying, I ended up being the only one sober enough to pick up Eric's sister, Marcia from the airport.

Taking over Eric's duties wasn't all bad. He was the groom, after all, and I was his best man and best friend since college. Besides, the drive from DC to Washington National Airport was short and pretty. The Potomac River sparkled in the dawn light and I got to drive Eric's brand-new convertible, which was convenient since I sold my car, along with my condo yesterday. I've got less than 48 hours in town before I catch a one-way flight to the one place I've always wanted to go—Ghana—to work on the project of a lifetime.

Besides, it was just as well that I face Marcia sooner rather than later. Marcia Champlain is not a terrible human being. She's smart, driven . . . attractive, even. It's just that ever since she graduated from high school, she somehow has it in her mind that we should be together, but the feeling is not mutual. Over the last 4 years, whenever I'm around her, I've tried to be subtle with my rejection. Unfortunately, Marcia is a lot of things, but being subtle is not one of them. At the barely there age of 17 ½, she asked her parents for a pre-birthday boob job that would take her natural 34B to a bodacious 34DD in time for her 18th birthday party. In a stunning display of overindulgence and crack-logic, her parents actually agreed to this. And ever since, Marcia seems to think that her DDs are the solution to every problem she faces. When she asked me out to dinner two years ago and I told her no, she literally thrust them into my chest and said, "Are you sure?" It took everything in me to keep from saying, "You know silicone and saline don't actually impair brain function, don't you?"

Although I've never been able to return Marcia's feelings, she's remained undeterred. The fact that I just happened to be the one escorting her down the aisle at her brother's wedding was undoubtedly another attempt to sway me. But it's all good. I could handle Marcia for one virtual day. Still, it was better to face the music and meet her head on so I'd know how to play it.

I decided to meet Marcia at the gate, hoping that the gesture would make up for any rejection I'd be forced to give later. But in retrospect, it was probably my first mistake of the day.

"Adam, you are *so* sweet," she called out while sashaying from the plane. "You look better and better every time I see you."

She went for the lips, but I gave her the cheek. I'd learned my lesson the hard way.

"How was your flight?" I asked while reaching for her carry-on.

"The usual. That two and a half hour flight from LA to DC is so boring, but you know Eric is too cheap to pay for the super sonic flight, so I had to slum it."

I nodded. It's hard to feel sorry for someone who's never had to pay for anything in her life. But I guess it wasn't entirely Marcia's fault. Spoiled and rich often went together, like entitled and privileged, careless and irresponsible. I was lost making similes when I realized she was speaking to me.

"Wait a minute. I think Eric mentioned that you've been going back and forth to Ghana to make some teleportation device that will zap us all from one place to another in no time."

I couldn't help but smile. I'd been obsessed with the notion of teleportation ever since my parents introduced me to Star Trek when I was seven.

"Yeah, a couple months ago I got selected as a team lead for the Teleportation Advancement Project (TAP). Me and about a hundred other scientists will be conducting the first experiments next Monday. Human trials are at least five years away, but we're making progress."

"You're just so impressive, Adam. You know, I could be your test subject, " Marcia said, stopping our slow walk to baggage claim. Her eyes were on me, batted and gooey.

"You'd have to move to Ghana for that," I replied with all the joy of knowing that this would never happen. "And besides, I don't think your brother would let me live if I atomized you."

Marcia's pretty face scrunched up.

"Ghana? You're moving to Ghana?"

"Yep, that's where all the experiments are going to be taking place, so I need to be there full-time," I replied, pleased that my "just got away with it" grin could be interpreted in many different ways.

Marica's frown deepened. "But, why? Why is this so important to you that you would leave your whole life here behind?"

"It's not just important to me. We're in the middle of a global energy crisis, Marcia and this project could be the key to ending it. If we're successful, it could reduce global energy consumption by more than 60%. We could bring desperately needed resources to places in the world that have been cut off due to the shortage, instantly. We could end hunger forever."

Marcia nodded solemnly. "You're right. It's just…Ghana is so *far*. When do you leave?"

"The morning after the wedding."

Marcia looked so disappointed that I almost started to feel bad, until her crestfallen sulk twisted into a mask of calculation.

"Is that so?" she cooed finally. Suddenly, she was all smiles again. "Well, I better freshen up. We don't have much time together, do we?"

Before I could respond, Marcia turned on her pencil-thin heels and headed to the ladies room. She glanced back and gave me a wink before disappearing behind a wall of blue-and-white tile. And as quickly as it came, my "just got away with it" feeling was gone.

Kea Brenner was Eric's fiancé and as a member of the bridal party, Marcia flew in to help with the final preparations. Kea was expecting Marcia to be dropped off at her house by 8:30am and I didn't plan to be a minute late.

After collecting two bags of luggage for a weekend stay, the trip to Kea's house wasn't nearly as tricky as I feared. These days it's rare to find a car you actually have to drive. Combustion engines and manual steering stopped being manufactured almost two decades ago. But if you have the money, you can customize your solar engine with a retro kit, with your choice of automatic or manual drive. The stick-shift option that Eric got for this car gave me a good excuse to keep an arm's length between us, blocking any attempts Marcia might make to place her hand on my thigh. Of course, she tried anyway.

It was no mistake that I made it over to Kea's place in record time. And just like the kind-hearted person that she is, Kea was standing at the front step waiting for us with a welcoming smile on her face. I dropped Marcia off with a wave and a pat on the back before getting the hell out of there. By the time I got back to Eric's house, the rest of the groomsmen were all awake, mostly alert, and fully resolved to start the day's activities. Tux rentals, haircuts, pictures, last minute errands, and then dinner with whomever of the wedding party were in town.

The day went by quickly, filled with rituals that seemed only half-necessary. We took our groomsmen pictures with dummies standing in for the bridesmaids we were supposed to be with. Everything would be spliced and manipulated later to incorporate the bridal party in our final images. It felt weird to me, but since everyone thinks I'm weird, that usually just means that this is all completely normal. By the time we arrive at the Asian fusion restaurant for dinner, I'm hungry and ready to settle in for a good time with some real food and real people.

There's something about being in a room where you know everybody. The vibe is like a low hum, with everyone on the same frequency. As a particle physicist, I study the connection between the real and the imagined all day long, but this is deeper than anything you can observe. It's not even something that you notice; you just feel it deep in your belly like a good wine, warming you from the inside out.

These are my friends. People I've shared my dreams with; people who have seen me triumph and fail - people who accepted a poor, nerdy kid from Philly into their decidedly cooler circle. Before Howard University and the people around this table, I never truly fit in anywhere outside of my family. I was confident in who I was, but reluctant to share myself with anyone. Looking in on my friends from the outside, it might appear that I still don't quite fit in. Of our rambunctious crew, I'm the least flamboyant, the quietest. Besides the fact that most of us are Black, around our table is every background imaginable - rich, poor, middle class, American, foreign, gay, and straight. In some ways, we have nothing in common, except our shared curiosity about life and a fierce love for each other. Our bonds were forged within the tension between struggle and laughter, secrets kept and shared, and the willingness to see and understand each other for exactly who we are.

In physics, we call it 'strong interaction,' the force that governs the clustering of all particles within the nucleus of an atom. It's always fascinated me the way the fundamental elements of the universe combine to form the most essential and the most frivolous things in our lives. Life expresses itself in an almost infinite number of variations, yet the basic building blocks of our existence are the same.

What is it that drives us towards some people and away from others? Is it emotional, cognitive, or some more urgent attraction between two opposite charges drawn to each other by an unbreakable law, a truth that cannot be undone. To me, it's magic, a mystery I've dedicated my life to solving. The pursuit of these questions led me to science, then particle physics. It led me to this wedding and all the beautiful, silly things I can and will never comprehend. I looked at Eric and Kea and marveled at all the elements and conditions that conspired to bring them together, and in the back of my mind, I wondered if those same dynamics would ever happen for me. But the answer to those questions could wait. So, I sat back as the love flowed around our table, erasing the lines between friend and kin, and listened to the familiar, effortless hum of us.

But in physics, it's always the disturbance, the introduction of a new element that opens up a whole new world of possibilities. So, when she tried to slip in discreetly, it didn't work. I felt it, *felt her*, immediately.

I had no idea who she was, this woman who came to an elegant dinner in a pair of blue jeans and a long sleeve T-shirt with a Chewbacca book bag slung over her shoulders. Even from the back, which was the only angle available to me, I could see that she was anxious. Her hands ran through her short hair nervously. She was talking to Kea in the small foyer of the restaurant, refusing to come in, even as Kea tried to pull her into the main dining area.

"It's fine. Girl, come on! We're just hanging out while we wait for the check. Come meet everyone," Kea encouraged.

It's hard to eavesdrop and play it cool, but I kept it together and tried my best to make out her voice over the *bossa nova* playing on the overhead speakers. As one of only a few solo guests for the evening, I sat at the edge of the table, which happened to be closest to the door and farthest from Marcia. It also gave me the best angle for listening in.

"Kea, I'm sorry. I just couldn't get out from under Professor Green tonight. I still have more papers to grade and . . . Look, never mind. I'll tell you about it later. Enjoy tonight. I'm so happy for you."

From the corner of my eye, I saw the strange girl lean in to give Kea a hug, not one of those half-cocked hugs where your elbows are more in than out, but a real 'wrap you in it' hug, an 'I mean it' hug. And I knew, despite not being able to see her face, despite having no idea who she was, that I liked her.

She left before Kea could even say a proper goodbye. When Kea returned to the table, I'd planned to ask who she was and if she was coming to the wedding tomorrow, but before I could put my plan in motion, everyone started to get up. Apparently Eric and Marcia's parents had paid for the whole thing and we were all headed out for the night. Kea never made it back to the table, so I never got to ask her who the girl with the Chewbacca backpack was.

By 10:00am the next day, we were all strapped into our pods, with the groomsmen and the bridal party hosted in two different quarters to "preserve the suspense."

Kea and Eric's parents sprang for the deluxe package, which included perks like IV feeds for inebriation, just in case you wanted to wake up from your virtual event as drunk as you thought you were and neural enhancers that were designed to make even the most mundane virtual sex seem amazing. I, of course, stuck to the basics. Neural enhancers could leave you disoriented and foggy in the worst way and even though I might have time to sleep it off on the seven hour flight from DC to Ghana, being out of it was just more drama than I needed.

Though Kea and Eric's parents had the resources to marry their children almost anywhere, Kea and Eric picked a place for the wedding that no longer existed in the real world, or if it did, human travel was strictly forbidden. The famous bayous of Louisiana were all but gone thanks to the effects of global warming. The same was true of several islands in the Caribbean and the Pacific. Twenty-five percent of the California shoreline had disappeared within a span of just three years and the great cities of Hong Kong and half of Manhattan were now underwater. It took these catastrophes for people to finally wake up. But once we did, the world got serious.

The New Delhi Accords for Global Regeneration were signed and ratified by the entire UN membership in less than a year. Instead of debating the extent of and culpability for global warming, nations jockeyed to lead the effort and bragged about their latest innovations in energy efficiency, conservation, and coastal restoration. Changes in behavior, manufacturing and policy that were thought to need years to take effect were implemented in months.

In the early days of the global conservation effort, restrictions on unnecessary flight travel were implemented, and with them, the virtual wedding industry was born, offering the experience of exotic locales for a fraction of the price of actually going there.

For a few more credits, you could even create a custom setting, constructed from your favorite book, time period or piece of art. For the right price, the neuro-techs would create anything you could imagine. And that's how we ended up in this fantasy made for two.

The theme for Eric and Kea's wedding was "Cotton Club on the Bayou"—a combination of scenes from Kea's favorite Louisiana mystery book series by Lynn Emery and Eric's flair for impeccable style. And as I stood in my virtual long-tail white tux at the edge of the placid water lapping at the riverbank, I had to admit that I was enjoying this fiction very much.

We stood there for a long while, Eric and all his groomsmen, just taking in the moment before the ceremony began. The perfume of lilacs, lilies and wisteria permeated the air around us, and though it wasn't real, I drank it in. Looking at my fraternity brothers to my left and my right, I noted that their faces were calm but serious. Each of us, in our own way, was embarking on a new journey: getting married, starting a family, launching a business, or ramping up for the next phase in our careers.

Even though I'd been on the teleportation project that led me to Ghana for over three years now, I felt it, too. A shift was happening in my life that was bigger than just moving to another continent, bigger than anything I had experienced in my life before, and I was ready for it.

When the first chords of the ceremony music began, we turned around and took our places in the staging tent. As the best man, I stood at the back of the line, making sure that I had Kea's wedding band securely tucked away. While the other groomsmen traded jokes and compliments with the bridesmaids, I practiced my ceremonial duties. I was in the middle of my fourth test-run of taking Kea's wedding ring in and out of my pocket without dropping it when Marcia found me.

"Put that thing away. You're too weird sometimes," she snapped. At the time, I remember thinking that she said 'weird' like it was a bad thing, but I kept that to myself. In a lighter tone, she added, "How do you like my dress?"

I tucked the ruby-studded wedding band inside my breast pocket and looked up to find her watching me with an exasperated expression on her face. Marcia was a pretty girl with a slim figure and curves everywhere that a woman is supposed to have them. Her dress was simple, off-white lace and strapless, which showed off her cleavage to great effect. In fact, it looked to me like she was kind of spilling out of it. Marcia didn't have to try nearly as hard as she did, but there was no telling her that.

"You look lovely," I said instead.

"Thanks," Marcia beamed, flipping her hair back as she took my arm. She leaned in to plant a sticky red-lipped kiss on my ear. Four-inch heels brought her close enough to my height so that we could stand almost shoulder-to-shoulder, and she used the opportunity to whisper incessantly in my ear throughout the entire march down the aisle.

By the time I got to Eric, I had tuned almost everything out just to keep my sanity, so when I looked up and saw a beautiful woman I didn't recognize standing with the bridal party, I was completely taken aback.

I had no idea where she came from or how I'd missed seeing her face before, but there she was, with warm brown eyes fixed on Eric and Kea and a smile that was gentle yet pensive. I immediately wanted to know what she was thinking. Her expression made me pay closer attention to what was happening with the ceremony just to see what it was that captivated her. As the pastor talked about the nature of - love, patient, kind, and never failing, I saw the corners of her eyes crease, and for an instant, she looked sad. Again, I wondered what memory or fear came to her in that moment.

This woman I'd never met before made me wonder so many things about her.

Complimented perfectly by the off-white color of her dress, her deep brown skin shown in the sunlight like polished ebony. Her shoulders and arms looked soft and supple to the touch. Then there was her face. Wearing easily less than half the makeup of anyone standing next to her, her features stood out so much more to me. Her eyes were large and shaped like plump almonds under the frame of strong black eyebrows. Her cheekbones were high, but hidden within the planes of her heart-shaped face, waiting to dazzle you when she smiled. Then there were her lips—curvaceous, full, and accentuated by only a hint of color.

To be honest, it was a struggle to avoid looking at her so that I could pay attention to the moment. I wanted to be there for my best friend who was starting a new life with the woman he loved. But by the end of the ceremony, the task was only half-done. I could feel my peripheral vision pulling in her direction with every chance my attention had to wander, until I would do almost anything to keep her there.

I saw Eric kiss his bride while still managing to keep her in my sight. By the time the newlyweds began walking hand-in-hand back down the aisle, I was on a mission.

I tracked her every step like a jealous lover. The sight of her smiling and chatting with her escort triggered some primal spot in my brain that had never been accessed before, and I'm not even that kind of guy, or at least I wasn't until that moment. To my right, Marcia was talking to me, complaining about how long the ceremony had been, but I couldn't even pretend to listen.
As soon as we returned to the staging tent, I watched a man I'd never seen before step up to the woman ahead of us and whisper in her ear. Emotions that I didn't even know I had were suddenly on high alert. I was ready to fight for no logical reason.

I don't even know her name, I thought in an attempt to reason with myself, but it was no use.

I dropped Marcia's arm, ready to bolt in between *her* and *him*, but he was closer to her than I was and I couldn't cross the distance fast enough. Before I knew it, they were walking off towards the reception area.

My mind was racing, trying to figure out what to do, when Marcia tugged on my shoulder.

"Not so fast. What are you, hungry or something?" I turned to the little sister of my best friend, keeping my mouth shut and my expression neutral for a very good reason. Undeterred as ever, Marcia pushed on. "I need to go to the bathroom. My feet are killing me. Wait right here."

Before I could tell her that I would do no such thing, Marcia was off. Immediately, I headed towards the reception area, determined not to lose track of my mystery woman again.

I found her and I saw him, laughing loudly and telling a joke that, by the lukewarm smiles around him, no one really thought was funny. In contrast, she stood slightly behind, yet beside him, sipping her drink quietly. It struck me as strange because I hadn't really gotten a "quiet girl" vibe from her. Her eyes during the wedding were lively and sharp, like she had a million thoughts in her head that she'd share for the asking. Watching her made me wonder how often she got asked to share them.

As they moved through the crowd, I noticed two things. One, they were obviously together in some arrangement that allowed him to be near her, yet did not require him to hold her hand or refrain from cutting her off in the middle of her sentences. The second thing I observed was that people clearly enjoyed interacting with her more than him. They leaned in closer, laughed longer, and touched more. She did the same.

Then there was the guy, hanging off of her like a piece of lint that no one had the heart to tell her about. Offensive, rude, and a total distraction from the beauty of her being—I could see everyone around her thinking it, but they didn't want to embarrass her, so they stayed polite. Unfortunately for him, I'd seen enough to know that I was just the one to pluck him right off.

I looked down at my drink, wondering if it was the cause of my sudden caveman tendencies. I didn't sign up for any neural perks while logged into the pod, but who knew. Unsure, I took another sip, just to test the theory.

I've never been a drinker, not really, but somehow in between staring at her and making small talk with people I couldn't even remember, I'd managed to get a drink in my hand. And the more I looked and sipped, the more I realized that what I was experiencing had nothing to do with the imaginary alcohol swirling in my glass. I felt unsettled, uncertain about where and who I was—things I never feel. I've always been certain. I was born certain. I have a t-shirt that says so. It's the nickname my fraternity brothers gave me the night I became an Omega Psi Phi.

I lifted the glass to my mouth and took another sip without even looking down to see what I was drinking. Cool with a hint of lime. I didn't care. I was just hoping it would somehow burn away the unsettled feeling in my stomach.

"Hey, C! Whoa, you're drinking? What's the occasion?" Eric asked while giving me a slap on the hand and a hug.

"No reason," I replied, bringing the glass to my lips. I bit down on ice cubes and watered-down liquor. My stomach was in knots.

I can't take my eyes off this girl.

"You all right . . . ?"

Eric's voice trailed off as he tracked my gaze. It didn't even occur to me to hide it. I saw him look back and forth between us before stepping directly into my line of view. Because I'm slightly taller than Eric, I could still see her just fine over his left ear, so I kept my eyes on him and tried not to smile.

"So, do you know Cara, or do you want to?"

His question gained my full attention, catching me off guard until I realized that the question itself was the problem.

Do I know her?

Yes, I wanted to say, but the truth was that I didn't, had never seen her before in my life. Except that wasn't true. I did know her. I just didn't know how or from where.

Cara. At least now I know her name.

"Is she a friend of Kea's?"

"Yeah, she and Cara grew up together in Columbia Heights, even went to the same - "

Just then, we were interrupted by a small group of his relatives that I knew almost as well as my own.

That's ok, I thought with a smile as I watched him get whisked away. *I'll find out when she tells me.*

So I watched, and the more I watched, the more she seemed to fidget while her boyfriend, or whoever he was, hovered over her like a rain cloud. I circled around, keeping to the edges of the party, where the fading sun didn't reach. It was crazy and I was aware of it, but the longer I did it, the more it seemed plausible that I could just *will* her over to me. Until, suddenly, she began looking around the room. At first, her glance was fleeting, as if she thought she heard someone call her name.

For some completely unknown reason, I slipped further back into the shadows. I remember thinking that I wasn't myself. Yet, while I didn't understand why I was doing what I was doing, I also didn't question it either. I stared at her is if I could see through her, understand her the way I wanted to, from the inside and out just by looking at her. She looked up again, sweeping the room with shaded eyes, and I knew that she could feel me. I had the strange sense that I was hunting her and it felt exactly right.

Does she know?

The thought that we could be so connected, that she could *feel* me near was profound. The notion left me feeling almost giddy, until the sound of Marcia's voice broke through my reverie.

"Adam, where have you been? I've been looking for you everywhere!"

Marcia's voice grated like a scratch over my favorite vinyl record. My trance was broken and as I turned to her, I felt myself slipping back into a normal that was somehow less than what it used to be. Then, from the corner of my eye, I saw my prey turn in my direction and look straight at me.

Damn.

I wanted to remind Marcia that we were not a couple, but I doubted that it would be of any use. By the possessive tone in her voice, I was pretty sure that she'd used our short time apart to start planning our wedding.

Last year, when Eric asked me to be his best man, I couldn't understand why he was so hesitant. We'd been best friends for years. We experienced college together. We pledged together. Being his best man was a given. But when I said yes, he didn't seem relieved.

"Of course," I assured him. "What did you think I was gonna say? I'm happy for you, man. You guys are perfect for each other."

"Ok, C, but listen. It's not my fault. Kea gets to pick her own maid of honor and she chose my sister, so there is nothing I can do about it." He didn't have to say another word.

Looking at Marcia, I realized that I was done trying to let her down easy. I needed to make sure that this was the last time she kept me from what I wanted.

"Did you need something?" I asked while taking a step back.

"You," she replied with a sly smile that made me want to shake my head.

"Marcia, I've told you. You're too young for me. I'm almost 30. You're barely 21. You need to find someone your own age. I'm sure there are plenty of guys around here who would love to get to know you."

"I need a man," Marcia declared, arching her back to close the distance between us with her favorite weapons of choice. I caught myself marveling at the interplay of mass and physics that kept her tiny frame from falling over.

Distracted, I responded without thinking, "And I need a woman. I don't belong to you, Marcia."

This time, my own words startled me. I wasn't dating. I didn't belong to anyone. So why would I say something like that?

The look of confusion on Marcia's face mirrored my own.

"Are you seeing someone else?" Marcia's voice was high and hurt. In frustration, I glanced to my right only to find that the woman I'd been stalking was no longer looking at me. Her eyes were cast to the ground in a studied indifference that wasn't quite convincing. Something was wrong and I couldn't help wonder if she'd seen this ridiculous exchange between Marcia and me and misunderstood.

I turned to Marcia and placed both hands on her shoulders. Surprised by the contact, she looked up at me with renewed hope, but I couldn't afford another second of this nonsense.

"Marcia, listen to me. We are not happening. Not now. Not ever. I need you to give up and move on."

Clean, simple. By the look on her face, I was satisfied that I'd made my point, but I have to say I didn't see the slap coming. It was strong enough to sting and loud enough to catch everyone's attention. All eyes were on us as Marcia stormed past me with a face too livid for tears. As I touched my cheek gingerly and watched her stomp away, I was relieved. If she had cried, I would have really felt bad.

I was pulled from the relief of my own small victory by the sound of the room erupting into cheers and laughter. From the way they were all looking at me, I assumed it was at my expense. But I don't mind, because in the middle of all those people was the one I wanted. She was looking at me again, but this time with a smile on her face and a small laugh that I could hear above every other sound in the room.

The joker beside her was on his phone, not even paying attention. He moved away from her, past me and into the hallway of the building behind us. I wasted no time making my move.

I walked up to her sheepishly, though inside I felt like a king, "Would you mind rescuing me? I think my ego needs a drink."

She laughed higher and it was all I wanted to hear. "Follow me," she said underneath all that chuckling. Her voice was sultry, deeper than I expected, but utterly feminine. It seemed familiar somehow, but I couldn't decide if that was just because I liked it. I fell in line easily, watching the hem of her skirt twirl as she walked.

"What did you say to her?" she asked when we finally reached the bar farthest from the scene of my public shame. "Girls don't like being rejected in public." A hint of her laugh was still there, but she tried to hold it back.

"I just told her the truth," I answered, leaning in a little. She smelled delicious, like she'd just stepped out of the shower.

"Maybe you should choose your words more carefully next time."

I heard her, but I was busy studying the lines of her face. I knew she was pretty. I could see that from clear across the aisle, but up close it was almost surreal. I could see the sweetness, the openness and the hunger in her eyes all at once. I was just about to get caught up in the curve that defined her upper lip when it occurred to me that I needed to say something in response.

"Sometimes you have to deal with something difficult to get to what is most important." I held her with my eyes, hoping that she would understand the thing I hadn't said.

For a second, I thought I saw it, but then she lowered her eyelids.

"What did you want to drink?" she asked, fiddling with a napkin at the bar.

"I think I'm good now."

Her pretty brown skin suddenly flushed, burgundy under the sepia of her cheeks. I didn't look away until she found the courage to meet my gaze.

"I'm Adam. Adam Coleman." I extended my hand hoping, *knowing*, she would take it.

"Cara," she replied, placing her hand in mine. "Cara Morgan."

I wanted to kiss it gently, but I didn't.

"You're the best man."

"Yeah," I replied, illogically thrilled that she knew that. "And you're Kea's childhood friend, right?"

"Right. Wait, if your name is Adam, why does Eric call you "C"?

"It stands for certain. It's the name my line brothers gave me when I became an Omega."

Cara's beautiful mouth slid to one side as she raised both of her thick eyebrows. It was clear that she thought I was full of it and for some reason, her reaction felt like coming home.

"And are you certain about everything?"

"Everything I want in my life, yes."

"Must be nice." I could hear the skepticism draining from her voice, so I went for it.

"It is. It helps me get what I want."

I felt myself grinning again for no reason other than her proximity. I wasn't sure if it was the fact that I kept staring at her or my answer to her question that seemed to make her slightly uncomfortable, but I couldn't help it if I wanted to.

Her eyes shifted away, but the burgundy in her cheeks told me that I was on the right track.

"Wasn't the ceremony beautiful? Kea and Eric are so perfect for each other." Cara's voice was softer as she tried to shift the conversation. She had no idea that wasn't even possible. I didn't just get slapped for nothing.

"They are," I began. "They put a lot of thought into every verse that was read, every vow. I could tell you were really paying attention."

"How?"

"Because I was watching you," I admitted. "I couldn't help it. The look on your face, it was like you were considering every word. I've heard Eric practice his vows a dozen times, but looking at you made me feel like I was missing something if I didn't listen to it again."

"Yeah." Cara's voice trailed off for a second. That pensive look on her face was back. "It's just . . . I don't usually like weddings these days, but Kea and Eric really made this one their own."

"Why don't you usually like weddings?"

"Oh . . . I do. I mean I don't like virtual ones that much. It's just kind of weird to me, but my mom says I'm old-fashioned, older than that even, but this one was really nice."

She laughed suddenly and the sound of it made me indescribably happy. "See, I'm a bad bridesmaid. I don't mean to sound like I'm complaining about the wedding."

"No, no, I understand completely. The whole 'virtual wedding thing' freaks me out, too. When I get married, I want it to be in a real place, with a real ring, even if it means that only the two of us are there."

Cara's eyes opened wide as she grabbed my hand and squeezed it tightly. I looked down to where our skin touched and felt a surge pass through me, stronger than when we first shook hands. I wondered if she felt it, too.

"Yes! I say that all the time," she began, clearly excited. "But Lyle . . ." She looked down at our hands, then slowly pulled away. "He . . . disagrees."

She might have been feeling timid, but at that moment, I was as far way from it as you could get.

"Is Lyle your boyfriend?" I already knew, but I wanted everything to be out in the open.

"Yes. He came with me. He's supposed to be around here somewhere."

I used the time she spent scanning the room to lean in again, savoring her scent and the way the tiny gold chain around her neck glistened in the fading sunlight. I didn't need to look around. I already knew he was nowhere near us. If he had been, he would have had the good sense to come get her before I stole her away for good.

"Well," I said, drawing her attention back to us. "Would you mind having dinner with me while you wait for him?"

She smiled then, so trusting and sweet that it cut whatever remaining boundaries I had with her wide open.

"Sure. I'd like that. Let's go eat some fake food!"

Once we'd given our toasts to the bride and groom, our conversation flowed easily as we sat together and talked through dinner and dessert. We watched in silence from the main dais as Kea and Eric took their first dance as man and wife. It was lovely and romantic, but all I could think about was being alone with her.

Lyle hadn't shown up yet, but by then, I don't think it would have mattered if he did. I knew she felt this thing between us as strongly as I did and I couldn't imagine that either of us would forget it. And then it hit me: what if she's in Tokyo or something?

Slowly, I shifted my eyes from the dance floor to her. To my left, Cara was leaning in to get a closer look at the bride and groom, so that when I turned my head, our faces were almost close enough to touch. I was afraid to ask, but I had to know.

"Cara, where are you right now?" I saw her look down and immediately, I knew that she'd been thinking about the same thing.

"I'm in D.C. Where are you?"

"Maybe about 100 feet away in the next room."

Her eyes light up so beautifully it made me chuckle.

"Really?"

"Yeah."

For a moment, we just stared at each other and it gave me all the courage I needed to ask for what I wanted.

"Cara, would you spend the night with me?" I could see her swallowing hard. I didn't know if that meant yes, but I leaned in anyway because she hadn't said no.

"I'm leaving tomorrow morning for Ghana, so my plan was to stay up tonight and just hang out in D.C. until my flight leaves. I don't know if you have plans later, but I'd love it if I could hang out with you."

For a long time, she didn't say anything, then she slowly placed her hand over mine on the table. Immediately, I felt it again, that rush of energy that courses through me every time we touch. After a moment, she looked up.

"I'd like that," she said softly, gathering a sliver of skin from the top of my hand. When I did the same to her, she smiled. In unison, we pinched each other and ended the simulation.

When I opened my eyes and slide from the Sim-pod, I'd never been so glad to be back in the real world. As I closed the door to the party pod and walked down the hall, I realized that I never asked Cara what she looked like or would be wearing. It wasn't uncommon for people to modify or change their virtual appearances so that, in the real world, they were practically unrecognizable from their virtual selves. She didn't seem like the sort of person who would do that but you never could tell. But just as

I rounded the bend that led to the main lobby, I saw something beautifully familiar.

Her short hair was even more tousled than yesterday as she ran her hands through it. And, though she wore a thin floral skirt that fell just above her knee and a white short-sleeve t-shirt, I knew who she was instantly. The Chewbacca book bag gave it all away.

The sound of my laughter must have made her turn around.

"Hi," she said shyly, extending her hand. "I'm Cara. It's nice to meet you for real this time."

"Absolutely," I replied and when I took her hand in mine, I felt the surge, stronger than I'd ever felt anything before.

※

"No, ma'am!" Adam said as he swatted my hand away from the fries on his plate. "Oh, I *see* how you are!"

Highland Café in Upper Northwest DC is famous among locals for its gourmet food and ample portions. I know how good their fries are. I eat them at least once a week, so I couldn't feel bad about trying to take a few for myself.

"What? You can't eat all that." I replied, more determined than innocent in my response. After all, Mo had only just served us our food.

"You must not know! I will *clean* this plate!" he said emphatically. To prove his point, Adam took an enormous bite of his burger, cutting it down by a third in just one take.

My hand hovered, waiting for a sign. He eyed me warily for a long while, until I began to realize that I might have found one of his deal-breakers, which made me really sad, because I love sampling other people's food. It's kind of a reflex/hobby of mine. But then, just as I was about to give up, he gave me a nod towards his plate. I stole two fries and stuffed them into my mouth before he had a chance to change his mind. Then, I remembered that he was watching. "Thank you," I mumbled through half-chewed food.

"I must really like you," he mumbled back before taking another bite of his burger.

I didn't even bother hiding my smile.

Adam drove us from the Sim Center to my house, where I decided we should ditch the car for the night.

"If it's your last night in DC, then we should walk it." I said. He agreed. Things were a little awkward in the car ride over, but once we hit the pavement, I felt like we could both breathe.

"I don't know about you, but I'm starving," he said. The way his eyes shown when he looked at me was addictive, so I tried to look away.

"Me too," I agreed. "I know a great place around the corner."

The walk to Highland's Café from my house took less than 5-minutes, and though it was crowded, Mo, the owner, spotted me and pointed out 2 seats at the bar that the people waiting for tables didn't want. We asked some folks to move down then squeezed in. That's what I love about this place. It's all about good atmosphere and good food. No airs. No drama. And breakfast all day.

The wait was long, but Adam was the best company I'd had in longer than I cared to think about.

After we ordered, he asked me what I did for a living and I told him that I'm an English professor at the University of the District of Columbia.

"Newly minted, so they give me all the work," I added. "I laugh, but I'm not joking. The memory of all the student papers I have to grade haunts me."

Adam looked at me with understanding. "Don't think about it. Not tonight," he said softly. As our drinks arrived, he rested his hand on my thigh. It lasted for only a second, but I felt it again, that warm energy that starts on the surface of my skin and seeps right down to the bone. It's delicious and unnerving all at the same time.

"But, I know what you mean," he continued. "Getting selected to TAP took about three years of serious grunt work, but it was worth it."

"I've been reading the science reports. It's amazing what you're doing. You must be so excited. You're making history."

His face took on an expression of child-like wonder that I hadn't seen from him until then and it made me like him even more than I already did.

"Honestly, Cara, it's more than a dream come true. It's surreal. My father named me Adam because he said that he knew I would be the first in whatever field I went into. So now, getting a chance to be a part of the International Science Team, having a chance to be among the *first* scientists to pioneer teleportation technology . . . it's just crazy. I'm blessed."

A comfortable silence spread between us then. And though I was a little in awe of him, I tried to keep it under wraps. *The last thing he needs is a fan girl following him around for the rest of the night.*

As if reading my mind, he changed the subject.

"But enough about me, what I want to know is why does an English professor follow science reports?"

"Well . . . I guess I'm just . . . kind of a geek. I have a lot of different interests; science is just one of them. Plus, I was curious how you guys were going to make sure that something bad didn't happen during the teleportation process, like that old movie my grandmother used to watch. What's it called again, the . . . ?"

"The Fly!" We said in unison. I laughed, while he groaned.

"That movie has been the bane of our team's existence since we started."

"Some might say it's a cautionary tale," I teased as Adam dropped his head on the counter in defeat.

"But it seems like you guys have a pretty good plan, from what I can tell—starting with something as simple as a coffee mug. I also read about the software you've developed to analyze and isolate particle groups so that everything isn't lumped together during the process."

Adam turned his head towards me, smiling. "Well, thank you. We're glad you approve."

"You're welcome. It takes a lot to impress a sci-fi fan."

Finally, he raised his head. "So, is that the answer to the mystery of your furry book bag?"

Now, it was my turn to groan. I'm always a little embarrassed walking around with my Chewbacca book bag, but my love for it always outweighs the looks I get.

"You think I'm weird, don't you?"

"Maybe, but I dig weird. There are worse things in the world than being weird," he declared before taking another enormous bite of his burger. Adam's plate was almost clean, while I'd barely made a dent in my Belgian Waffle breakfast platter. I shook my head and laughed.

"Oh yeah, like what?"

He looked up from his plate with an intensity that surprised me. "Not being yourself."

His words made me want to cry, but I focused on finishing my food instead. He got the check while I finished up, watching me eat the entire time.

"You're shy, aren't you?"

"Sometimes," I answered truthfully.

"Well, you're going to have to get over that tonight, because I want to know everything there is to know about you, Cara Morgan."

I chewed my food and swallowed hard, not because I thought he was lying, but because I knew he wasn't. And even more than that, I knew I would tell him anything and everything he asked me.

After Highland's, we headed down Fourteenth Street. I took him past the first house my great-grandparents bought and renovated in DC, back when they were immigrants from the Islands who had just graduated from Howard University. As we weaved in an out of the tree lined streets and cracked pavement, I shared the history of the Columbia Heights neighborhood that I grew up in as it was told to me by my grandmother.

From Columbia Heights, we crossed over to 16th Street and headed into Meridian Hill/Malcolm X Park where an impromptu Go-Go session was already underway. By that time, it was well after midnight, but nobody cared.

Bodies swayed to the drumbeats as they moved from Go-Go to samba to African rhythms older than anything standing in our midst. To my utter shock, during a transition in the play, Adam sat down among the musicians, took up one of the paint can drums not being used, then kept the beat with the other drummers. As he played, I saw that kid-like joy that I glimpsed earlier—equal parts happiness and quiet reverie with a touch of mischief that turned everything he did into something sexy. There in his grey t-shirt and blue jeans, with his black and white sneakers on, he could easily have been mistaken for just another young man on the street, and I had a feeling that he kept it that way on purpose. By the time he got up from the session, he was slightly sweaty and beaming. I could smell his cologne even more than I had before. The scent of him was warm and heady.

"You didn't know I had those kinds of skills, did you?" he said, proudly throwing an arm around me. I leaned in to him even more because he smelled so damn good.

"Where did you learn that?"

"Come on now. I'm a Howard man and an Omega Psi Phi," he said cryptically, as if that should explain everything.

By one o'clock, we were hungry again, so we stopped off for a bite to eat at Afterwords, a café inside an old-fashioned bookstore in Dupont Circle that stayed open until 4am. The detour turned into an hour and a half-long discussion on books and films that we loved and hated.

By three am, we were headed to the Mall to see what was left of the cherry blossoms, talking the whole way down. And somewhere between the jokes and the laughter, the revelations and quiet confessions, I realized that this man whom I'd only just met already knew more about me than Lyle or almost any other adult I knew. The more I talked, the freer I felt, and the freer I felt, the more afraid I became. I could feel the butterflies rising in my stomach.

By the time we reached the Mall, Adam was holding my hand. All around us the cherry blossoms were in full bloom, glowing, soft pink petals in the moonlight. We stopped at my favorite spot on the Tidal Basin, where you can take in the Washington and Jefferson Memorials, and the FDR Monument with only a slight turn of your head.

Leaning against the painted grey rails, I looked out onto the water and took a deep breath of the cool night air. I could feel him behind me, hovering for only a second before he offered me the warmth within his arms. The rush was overwhelming.

The skin on his arms felt like satin against mine, and I found myself reveling in it. I was going to tell him something about the paddleboats to our right and how as a child, my father used to take my friends and me out to ride them, but the silence around us felt sacred and I didn't want to break it.

Looking down at our arms wrapped around each other, I noticed that my skin was darker than Adam's, but not by much. In the night that surrounded us, you could barely tell the difference and I was mesmerized by the way our skin blended together. When his lips brushed against the back of my neck, the sheer pleasure of it made me shudder.

In response, he held me closer, tight enough to send the butterflies in my stomach into a frenzy of anticipation. But I locked myself in place, resisting the urge to turn around and bring him closer, though the impulse was all consuming. My heart raced as the realization came like the sharp taste of adrenaline in my mouth. Any attempts to turn back now would be useless. If I'd wanted to save myself from loving him, I shouldn't have agreed to leave the wedding, because by then I knew, didn't I? Hell, I probably shouldn't have agreed to rescue him from Marcia.

But it was too late for any of that. His arms were around me, and while I couldn't turn around, I was certain it was no longer in my power to let go.

"Why are you holding back from me?" he whispered against the skin on my collarbone. "Don't you know what this is?"

The heat from his body lulled me into him. I leaned back into him helplessly, even as my lips quivered with the truth.

"Because I'm scared."

"Come here, girl," he whispered before turning me around and enclosing me again in his embrace. I pressed closer and rested my head on his chest, because I knew I belonged there, and fighting it didn't make it any less true. I could feel his voice rumbling through his chest as he spoke.

"It's just us, sweetie. There's nothing to be afraid of. It's just us."

This is all too soon. Over and over, I told myself, *I don't do things like this. I don't fall in love so easily. I barely know him.* But the other truth was even scarier – that in this moment—I barely knew myself.

And then there was Lyle. Even though he'd disappeared at the wedding, he was still my boyfriend. I've never been the kind of girl who cheated. That just wasn't my thing. But what could I say now? Thinking of him felt suspiciously convenient, like a tool I was using to create a distance between Adam and me that should have existed, but didn't. The truth was that nothing in me felt even the slightest guilt about being with Adam. Everything about us felt more immediate, more real then any other relationship I'd ever had, even though it made no sense for me to feel that way.

This is all too soon.

So, I grabbed onto the fact of Lyle as the only logical thought that had passed through my head the entire evening.

With determination, I forced my arms to let go of Adam and push myself away.

He only allowed me to move as far as the length of his arms around me.

"I have a boyfriend," I said, with my head low. "I shouldn't be here with you like this."

Adam removed one hand from my back and brought it to my chin, raising my head slowly, until I was forced to face him. When I finally met his gaze, his eyes were gentle, but dead serious. He brushed a lock of hair behind my ear.

"His time with you is over. You shouldn't be anywhere else but here."

I stared at him, stunned by the simple truth in his words. I wondered how he made them true, how I already knew that he was right.

And when he kissed me, his lips were soft and wet like rain. I swallowed him whole, every drop I could get until I was weak with the need to be consumed. When my knees buckled he pulled me to him. Strong arms kept me close as his tongue slide against my mouth.

I felt it everywhere.

By the time he slipped inside, I'd become this moaning, grasping, spasming thing. Places in me were calling to him that I didn't even know had voice. I pressed closer, knowing that any part of me he touched would ignite.

And I learned everything I never knew, all at once.

How a man kisses a woman.

How a woman devours her mate.

How we love.

How we love.

He pulled away from me shaking, with a wild, happy look on his face that mirrored my own.

"Damn." His breathing was ragged as he pressed his forehead into mine. Slowly, Adam's hand followed the curve of my spine up to my neck. Fingers moved into my hair, massaging my scalp until he gathered the strands at the base of my skull into a fist and pulled, just a little, just enough.

Something inside me fell away as he moved my head back so we stood face-to-face.

I looked at him with clear, wanton eyes, knowing that he saw everything that I craved in that moment. I tried to move forward, to seize the curve of his lip, but he held me in place by my hair.

"I want you," I said. My voice was half growl, half-moan, and wholly unfamiliar to me.

"You have me, Cara. You already have me."

He took his time, staring unflinchingly into my eyes. I wondered if he could see everything I was feeling: the insatiable abyss of my desire, all my loneliness and doubt, my longing, all the places I'd waited a lifetime for him to touch.

I didn't realize I was crying until he wiped away the tears.

"Shhh. You're beautiful to me. Don't cry, baby. I don't think I can stand it," he said, crushing me to him.

I felt exposed, naked except for the warmth of his embrace. But the feeling of safety was so unfamiliar to me that I fought it.

"I'm not sure I'm up for this," I said. It was and it wasn't true. I wanted to resurrect my defenses, but I couldn't find them anywhere. Feeble words were all I had.

"We were made for this," he whispered. I could hear the same ache I felt in his voice. "There's nothing else but this. I know you know it. I see it when I look at you."

When he kissed me again I could taste the salt between us, the desire that was so much more than just mine. Without words, there was nothing but the knowing of what this was and what it had to be. I leaned into it with all my might, wrapping my arms around him and pulling him closer, until he lifted me up onto his hips and carried me off the path and into the trees.

My hips moved on their own accord. I moaned into his mouth as I felt his length between us, and as I pressed against him, Adam moaned right back. I knew what I wanted to happen, but it's only when I felt my back up against a tree that I found the courage to say it.

"Make love to me. I want to," I whispered in between breathless kisses.

His mouth stilled, then hovered close enough for me to feel his words when he spoke.

"Cara, I'm leaving in the morning," he said before beginning a slow trail of kisses down my neck.

"I don't care. I want to know what this feels like, just once . . ."

In response, his hips ground into me hard, pressing my body flush against the tree.

"Not just once," he whispered roughly into my ear before unwrapping my legs from around his waist and placing them on the ground. Before I could look up, Adam whirled me around so that he was behind me with my body pressed into his chest. His lips at my ear sent a shiver down my spine.

"I could never have you just once," he whispered as one hand raised up to cup my breast.

"The next time I see you." The fingers of his other hand slipped past the hem of my skirt and into my underwear. "The first thing

I plan to do is make love to you." His thumb swirled around my most sensitive place, while two other fingers went deeper.

With our bodies pressed heavily into the tree, he held me up and kept me in place.

"I plan to take my time." The motion of his fingers was slow, but firm. He'd only just started, but it was already the most sensual experience of my life and I could feel myself coming undone.

"I plan to show you that 'just once' does not apply to us." As my arms and legs began to tremble, I held on to his thigh and the back of his neck, trying to keep myself upright so he could finish what he started.

"I'm not going to take you now because I'm not going to remind you of any other man you knew before me. Someone else who touched you, then broke your heart. When you think of me, I don't want to share that space with anyone else. Do you hear me, Cara? Do you feel what I'm saying?"

I nodded because I couldn't speak. There were too many things happening to me that had never happened before.

"I intend to love you, Cara," Adam continued, as his strokes became deeper and slower. I could feel myself—senseless, shameless, and completely open—teetering on the edge of complete surrender. "As soon as you let me, for as long as you let me. Let me," he whispered. "Let me."

And when I finally gave in to the truth of his words and the strength of his fingers, there was only bliss.

※

I woke to his lips pressed against mine, feather-light and sweet. When I opened my eyes, Adam was staring back at me with a sad little smile. All around, the morning sky was opening up in shades of pale yellow and blue. I was instantly awake.

"What time is it?" I asked, feeling the car seat against my bottom.

"It's 6:18."

"Your flight leaves at 7:30. We have to get to the airport!"

"We're already here, sweetie. I just . . . didn't want to stop watching you sleep."

"Won't you miss your flight? They still have to scan you before you board."

"As a member of the International Science Team, I don't have to be scanned."

"What about your luggage?"

"I don't have any. All my stuff was shipped a week ago," he replied. "Besides, the one thing I want to take with me won't fit in a carry-on."

I looked down at my hands where he held them, fighting back tears. There were so many things unresolved in my life, yet none of them seemed more important than not letting go of his hand.

"Can I ask you something?"

Please don't ask me, I begged silently. *If you ask me, I don't know how I'll have the strength to refuse.*

"Adam, please . . ."

"Just one thing. It's a small thing. I promise." The mischief in his voice made me look up.

"So . . . can I ask you?" His smile was broad and infectious. I nodded. "Will you walk me to the gate?"

When my mouth fell open in surprise, he laughed. "See, that wasn't so bad, was it?"

I narrowed my eyes, then punched him in the arm.

He was right about security. Even with me in tow, with no bags, it took less than 15 minutes to get to the gate. Still, by the time we got there, I was stunned to find that they were already boarding.

"Listen," Adam began as he took my face gently between the palms of his hands. "I love you. I know it's too early to say it, but I do. If I could, I would stay here with you. Despite everything that's riding on this experiment, I would stay, but there is too much at stake for our future and too many people counting on me to just think about how wrong it feels to walk away from you.

"I…" his voice trailed off for a moment before Adam reached into his back pocket and pulled out a small blue napkin from Highland's Cafe. "This is where I'll be. No matter what I'm doing, call this number and someone will get ahold of me. Come find me, Cara. When you're ready to let me, I'll be waiting."

Taking the napkin from him, I blushed, remembering us under the cherry blossoms. Our last kiss was brief, but I felt it long after he said goodbye and turned to leave.

I watched his plane take off and followed it until it disappeared into the clouds. Despite having only just met him, I sat at the departure gate long after he'd gone and wondered what I was doing there without him.

I've always been the kind of person who gets completely immersed in my work. The TAP program is one I've wanted to work on for years. As a grad student and doctoral candidate, I volunteered thousands of hours to work on TAP under my professor and mentor, Dr. Nkrumah until finally, I earned the attention of those in a position to hire me on the project.

But to be chosen as part of the team to perform the first teleportation experiments was beyond my wildest dreams, even though I worked for it and hoped for it for the better part of three years. So to be sitting in a first class seat on a supersonic jet on my way to Accra, Ghana with Cara as the only thing on my mind pretty much says all you need to know about what this woman I just met means to me already.

But I heard her loud and clear last night as she told me about her three-year relationship with Lyle. She had made a lot of compromises in her career and her personal life to make it work with him. I didn't want her to have to do the same for me. I wanted us to be her choice—to define the terms of how we would work for herself. So I didn't ask her to come with me, even though I wanted to, even though I'd already reserved a ticket for the seat next to mine while she slept. I've never been a patient man, but this was worth waiting for. She was worth waiting for.

The first thing I did when I made it to the lab was log Cara in as a primary person of contact, which meant that when she called, they would know it was a priority. Then I scrubbed in. Everything (or anyone) who enters the teleportation chambers has to be sterilized to minimize the amount of dust and organic material the sensors will have to decipher and isolate in order to facilitate a successful transfer. The reason is simple: we don't have the computing power to detect and analyze complex organic tissue. As one of the project leads, my team is responsible for calibrating the particle sensors and developing the software necessary to quantify whatever they pick up. In other words, our team's job is to make sure that we catch whatever the teleporter absorbs so that it can be reassembled on the other side.

It's detailed work, tedious and exacting, but I can't deny that I love the precision, the idea that everything I did helped to ensure our success as a team. The more diligent I was, the more likely it was that we would meet our goals. Plus, the work helped to keep me from going crazy with the memories of everything Cara and I shared. After all, the first TAP trials were less than two days away, and I needed to focus.

We worked almost around the clock, checking and re-checking every switch and every software simulation. The atmosphere at the lab was intense, reverent even, but still a little giddy. We were all aware that we were on the verge of something historic, no matter what happened.

Similar to the design of the Large Hadron Collider that was built in Geneva more than 40 years ago, the teleportation chamber was designed to withstand the bombardment of particles traveling at high speeds. But in our case, instead of hadrons, we were using weighted light particles called m-photons and traveling at the speed of light. The idea is to hit whatever we're trying to transport so fast and with such intensity, that rather than decomposing, it shatters into its fundamental elements, which are then recorded, absorbed, then re-assembled into the receiving chamber just 50 feet away.

If we're successful, we will change what it means to transport and travel forever. Distance, like the miles between Accra and Washington DC, will become irrelevant. I could be with her in an instant. But we're not there yet, so we started with something simple, a plain white coffee mug that our team affectionately named Jo.

But first we had a little party that lasted well into the wee hours of the morning.

On testing day, my job was to take a reading of all the sensors to gain a baseline of conditions in the chamber. This would enable our computers to distinguish, then group elements that should be together so that the air particles in the chamber don't become a part of the cup we're teleporting. The baseline read is taken as close to the teleport as possible to make sure that we have the most accurate picture of the environment within the chamber before teleportation takes place. Everything looked good until I decided to do a random check of the floor sensors one more time, just to be sure.

The sensors picked up traces of aluminum that's not supposed to be there and some residue made of yeast, barley and saliva. Suddenly, everyone's frantic, trying to model out in their heads how the compounds could've gotten into the chamber. I figured it out first. Not because I'm smarter than everyone else. I just happened to know about alcohol and its effects on human behavior more than most in the room. I am, after all, a frat brother.

The TAP experiment is on a timer because it takes time to accelerate particles to the speed of light. And once they reach maximum velocity, nothing human can stop it. The main reason we picked the cup is because it has no organic material. There are trillions and trillions of atoms in the human body, which would require a teleportation computing capacity that we are years away from having. Even a drop of saliva contains too many complex particle variables for us to reliably contend with. The metal we can compensate for, but anything organic is out.

I looked at the clock. We had less than ten minutes until photon impact.

"It's beer," I announced bluntly while looking around for the culprit. "Someone was in the chamber last night with a beer."

The notion that any one of us would be stupid enough to do this was almost inconceivable, but I knew I wasn't wrong.

Sweaty-faced and beet-red, it wasn't hard to pinpoint the offender.

Colin Moss was an intern in his second year of grad school physics. With a course work average of B-, he shouldn't and wouldn't have been here, except his father donated a billion dollars to this effort. I could easily imagine the selfie he would have taken in the chamber.

We made eye contact, but I quickly looked away and began unbuttoning my lab coat. With less than nine minutes before impact, I resolved to fix the teleporter problem first and chew him out later.

"Adam, where are you going?" Dr. Bain, head of TAP operations, asked while following me out of the control room.

"The sensors pinpointed the droplets. I'll be in and out in three minutes. If I can't find the aluminum, it doesn't matter. Our systems can isolate it. We just need to get the organic material up."

She stared at me while I put on my gloves and grabbed a sterile suit. I got dressed while she thought it over. By the time she came to the same conclusion I had, I was all zipped up.

Six minutes before Photon-Impact, the project timer announced.

"Hurry, Adam," she said, and handed me the sanitizing solution.

There are two doors that I had to pass through to make it into the chamber. One sanitizes, the other neutralizes the electrical charges on my suit. Finally, I passed through and opened up the chamber doors that sealed me in once I reached inside.

I would never have found the droplets on my own, but I'm synced to my computer with a clear picture of where to go. So when I saw the spot location super-imposed on my helmet screen, I knew exactly where to find them. I knelt down, sprayed, and wiped it clean. I had two minutes left.

Just like cleaning up the frat house before the headmaster comes through for inspection, I thought. *"Experience is knowledge."* Einstein would be proud.

By the time I'd cleaned up the mess and turned towards the chamber door, I was smiling and pretty satisfied with myself. I placed my hand on the scanner embedded in the chamber door. It was supposed to open automatically from the inside, but it didn't. Surprised, I tried to give it a shove, but it wouldn't budge. I could hear its delicate gears trying to open, but nothing happened.

Dr. Bain opened up the communication link in my helmet. "Adam, get out of there. Photon impact is in one minute and twenty seconds."

"I'm trying, but it's jammed."

In the background, I heard my mentor, Dr. Nkrumah, yelling, "Get him out of there, now!"

Sixty seconds to photon impact.

Chaos erupted in my ears as everyone started running around, denying what I already knew.

The teleportation chamber door is designed to hold things in: light, matter, any lethal explosion that might occur. Yet it's delicate enough to act as a kind of sensor of its own, recording every particle it encounters.

Fifteen seconds to photon impact.

I backed away from the door. My mouth was dry, but my eyes were sharp. The world around me looked so clear to me in that moment as my brain filtered out everything, except for the sound of my own thoughts, and that's when it occurred to me.

The metal . . .

10 seconds.

Maybe it's a beer can lid . . .

9 seconds.

. . . lodged into the door gears

8 seconds.

. . . in just the right way.

7 seconds.

My mind went silent with the irony . . .

6 seconds.

. . . of all my diligence undone.

5

And what . . .

4

. . . will I

3

. . . become now?

2

My only other thought . . .

1

. . . was of Cara.

Impact

From somewhere outside myself, I saw my body explode into a trillion shards of light and become everything and nothing all at once.

I rode back from the airport more awake and more alive than I had ever felt before. With the car on auto-pilot, I stretched out in the backseat and wrote everything about our first night together in the journal that I kept in my book bag. I wanted to document it so that when I saw Adam again, he could read it and know all the things he awakened in me. I wanted to record it so that when our children read it, they would understand how strong and how beautiful real love comes.

After programming my car to meet me at Eric's house in the posh, gated community of Anacostia, I left his car in the driveway and took my own back home. With barely any traffic, I made it back to my house in no time. The yellow house with the white front porch has been in my family for two generations. Sometimes it was rented out. Sometimes a relative would move in, but it has always stayed in the family.

Though I hadn't eaten in hours, I wasn't hungry. Instead, I took a shower, slipped on a T-shirt and slept for five hours with the feel of his lips still haunting my skin. I dreamt of him waking up next to me. In my dream he said nothing, but we smiled at each other with the kind of joy that needs no words. I woke missing him so much it hurt to breathe. When the pain subsided, I rolled over, ready to close my eyes just for another chance to see his face again, but before I could get there, my mother's face appeared on my home communication link. I reached over with a smile to connect the call.

"Cara! Where have you been? I've been calling you on your link since yesterday to see how the wedding went, but it said that your link was off. You never turn your link off, not even when you're teaching. Then I really got worried when Lyle called. He said he left your side for just a second at the wedding to take an urgent phone call and when he got back you were gone. He said he heard that you left with some guy?"

Lying to my mother was not something that I took lightly, but I decided to shake it off.

"Mom, relax. Sorry I worried you, but I'm fine. I promise."

And then I told her all about Adam and our night together. When I voiced my plans to figure out a way to be with him, I thought she would be hesitant, but as always, she surprised me. Instead, Mom was thrilled beyond belief.

"Oh, and he's so handsome. Look at those eyes!" I saw her smile grow as she used the global search function on her screen to look him up. "And good teeth, too! I can't stand a man with an ugly mouth. Now, your father, he has an excellent set of teeth."

"Are you serious right now, mom? Teeth, that's the secret to a good man?" I laughed in that way that only my mother can make me.

"It worked for me," she said, grinning.

"I love you, Momma," I began, just as Lyle's face popped up on the bottom right of my screen.

"Hey, this is Lyle on the other line. I've got to talk to him." I reached over and activated the keyboard to send him a message letting him know I would switch over in a minute.

"You better," he wrote back. I had to smile. Whoever said breaking up is hard to do never dated Lyle Fisher.

"Well, don't let him give you any trouble over this. Just drop him quick and be done with it. I never liked him anyway." My mother spared one moment for an exasperated expression before returning to her good mood.

"Is that how you did your break ups?" I asked with a smirk. My Mom is as sweet as pie until you cross her, then watch out! That five foot tall woman turns into an eight-foot beast.

"Cara, I was worse than that! You're a lot nicer than I was. In my day, I'd send them a text, then change my phone number."

She had me laughing so hard I was almost in tears.

"Oh Mom, I *am* nicer than you, but I've got to go. I love you."

"Love you too, dear. And call me back when you're done with that fool so I can get the details on *Dr.* Coleman."

"All right," I said shaking my head.

When I clicked over, Lyle got straight to the point. "Where the hell have you been?"

So I decided to do the same. "Lyle, it's over."

"What!" His expression seemed genuinely surprised and, for a second, I actually started to feel bad, but then he opened his mouth and absolved me of all my guilt.

"Is this about that guy you left with? What happened? You give him some tail and lose your mind?"

"Lyle, whether I did or didn't sleep with him is none of your business anymore. You don't love me. I don't love you."

"You don't love me? Since when? You're the one always talking about marriage and babies and—"

"Since right now," I answered back, then severed the Com link.

Knowing he was likely going to call back (or worse, come over), I made the decision to do one of my favorite things—take an impromptu drive to Assateague Beach. I packed all the papers I had to grade, two books, a bathing suit, two sundresses, deodorant, some underwear, and my toothbrush and was out of the house and on the road in ten minutes.

The drive took about three hours, which gave me time to cancel my afternoon class, book my favorite bed and breakfast, call my mother back, and think about what this new life I wanted to create looked like.

I started to call Adam, but stopped myself before the connection was complete. I realized then that when I spoke to him next, I wanted a plan. He'd given me his love, now I needed to give my commitment, but for that, I would have to give myself something I'd never allowed myself to have before—time to figure out exactly what I wanted. Before, I'd rushed in to relationships, always worried that the men who said they loved me would change their minds and turn away. But I didn't have to do that with Adam. Because of him, I felt certain that I wouldn't have to do that with anyone ever again. The memory of us easily extended out into plans. From my perch on the beach, I could see everything I wanted for our lives together. And for the first time, I wasn't worried about whether or not he would approve. I knew he would. We were meant for this.

Let me, he whispered in my ear, and I intended to.

For the next two days, I was blissfully isolated, lost in the dream of our future together. So that on Monday, I was completely caught off guard when I woke up screaming, jolted awake from a nightmare that began as a beautiful vision.

In the dream, Adam and I were walking along the beach, retracing the path that I had taken every morning for the last two days – right at the shoreline, where I could feel the waves lapping at my feet. As we walked, Adam told me about his parents.

"When I come back," he'd said, "I'll take you to meet them."

"I'd like that," I answered, smiling up at him until his expression shifted from carefree joy, to concern, then panic.

"Adam! What's wrong?"

He looked down at his feet and as my gaze followed his, I saw the waves reach up, bubbling over his feet and ankles until they dissolved then receded with the tide. There was no blood, no bone, only pieces of him fading into sand and water as the stains from the seawater crept up his pants leg. Drops of water fell down, taking more pieces of him away.

With desperate eyes, he looked up at me. His voice was a whisper. "I can't move. I can't get out…"

"Adam!" I screamed as the waves engulfed us, higher and stronger. Suddenly, I was pulled out to sea while the waves at the shore rose up to encircle him until he was finally washed away. Desparate, I fought through the cauldron of frigid water, searching for him in the deep, endless blue, but I could not find him anywhere.

"Adam!" I woke up screaming his name into the stillness of early morning light, but nothing answered back.

I felt instantly sick.

It was only a dream, I told myself, *only a dream*, but the tears came anyway. With the chill of the water still on my skin, I couldn't stop shaking, couldn't get the image of him fading away out of my mind. The ache in my chest came next, like a black hole growing within me where my heart used to be. Unable to stop crying and unable to breathe, I forced myself from the bed, stretching my chest out as if to force the air inside. Standing helped, but only a little.

"All I have to do is call him," I told myself. The sound of my voice saying the words out loud was reassuring and calmed me enough to walk into the sitting room area of my bedroom suite and look for the book bag that held my com-link. My hand trembled as I reached for it, but I tried my best to ignore it. As I activated the device, my schedule came up as I'd programmed it to do every time I turned it on.

TAP Experiment – 8am EST

Damn it!

I'd set-up the notice on my phone two days ago, then promptly turned off my phone to avoid the sound of Lyle's calls going to voicemail. I'd forgotten to turn it back on last night, which was why my alarm didn't go off this morning. Looking at the time, I shook my head in disgust. The experiment, if successful, would take less than 30 seconds to complete.

"The test has been over for 20 minutes now. He's probably celebrating or holding a press conference. There's no way I'm going to be able to talk with him now."

Annoyance felt better than the lingering fear from my dream, so I clung to it as I threw my link on a nearby chaise and crossed the room to turn on the TV. If I can't talk with him, at least I can see his face, I thought.

"Commercials…," I murmured. When I couldn't get away from the advertisements being featured on every channel, I decided to head to the bathroom until the news returned. I was in the middle of washing my hands when I overheard the words 'tragic' and "Dr. Coleman"

Running back into the sitting room, I watched as the newscaster talked beside a professional photo of Adam standing in a white lab coat outside of the TAP facility in Accra.

"Dr. Adam Coleman completed his Doctorate in Particle Physics at MIT and had been working with TAP for over 3 years. He was just 29 years old and while we understand that he was not married, both his parents are still alive and have been watching the horrific events of this morning unfold from his childhood home in Philadelphia.

"Though we've invited Mr. and Mrs. Coleman on the air to speak with us, they are understandably unable to do so at this time. They do, however, ask that we continue to pray for a solution to the impossible predicament that their son now finds himself in.

"For those of you just joining our broadcast, at 7:58 am EST Dr. Coleman was trapped inside the teleportation chamber and atomized at the TAP facility in Accra after a routine systems check turned up a small trace of organic material. Dr. Coleman went into the chamber to address the problem when the door locked behind him and was apparently jammed from the inside. TAP scientists continue to report that they have no way to bring Dr. Coleman out of suspended animation. We will now play a video of the accident as it occurred at the TAP facility this morning. We warn you that some of the images you're about to see may be disturbing."

I don't remember hearing anything else after that. I only remember watching the images of Adam from my dream being played out again in front of me. Although the water in my dream was replaced by a beam of light, the image of him being consumed by a force of nature was exactly the same.

And just like in my dream, he was gone.

The ache in my chest ripped open and brought me to the ground like a piece of fallen silk. I stayed there as the newscaster continued telling a story that I realized I already knew.

In my head, I heard his voice reaching out to me, telling me not to cry, that he couldn't bear to see me so sad. His voice was so strong that it felt like more than memory. Almost, as if – if I had the courage - I could open my eyes and find him lying on the floor right next to me.

The very notion was torture, turning my tears into sobs so loud that Mrs. Pierce, the innkeeper, came pounding at my door.

But I didn't get up. I couldn't get up.

I don't want to hurt you, he pleaded. *I don't want to hurt you.*

Then come back to me, I whispered, but the voice in my head offered no reply.

By the time I made my way to the bedroom door, Mrs. Pierce had comeback with a key to my room and my mother on the other end of a handheld phone.

"I didn't know what else to do," Mrs. Pierce admitted as she looked me over in the doorway.

"Your mother was the only person listed under your emergency contacts and when you didn't answer, I just…." I must've really looked a mess because before I could offer an apology for my behavior, Mrs. Pierce just handed me the phone and turned away. I closed the door behind me and braced myself against it before bringing the phone to my ear.

All it took was the sound of my mother's voice whispering, "I'm so sorry, sweetie" for me to sink to the floor and begin crying all over again.

I couldn't face the drive home, so I booked the room at my Bed and Breakfast for two more days. All the happiness, all the hope I'd felt coming here had disintegrated, piece by piece, with Adam. By midday, I couldn't stand to watch the news anymore and hear one more time how hopeless the situation was. I went to bed at 5 pm that night with a barely eaten box of cookies and a bottle of water on my nightstand, but sleep offered no escape from sadness. I tossed and turned all night trying in vain to get close to the image of him I refused to let go of in my mind. In my dream, I saw him like a mirage floating in the same water that swept me away. He was trying to swim towards me, but the tide kept pushing us apart.

I woke up in the middle of the night with tears streaming down my face and my throat raw from screaming his name. Whether it was from grief or exhaustion, I don't know, but somehow I fell back to sleep, lulled by the feel of Adam's presence beside me. In desperation, I focused my every thought, my every prayer on my need to hold him there until I wept at the delusion of feeling his hands running through my hair.

I'm delirious, I thought.

It doesn't matter, I heard him say. *You're dreaming*.

Early the next morning, I woke up drained, but with a strange sense of calm. Forcing myself to get up, I walked to the bathroom, still exhausted and in no shape to work. But I knew life wouldn't stop just because I wanted it to. My students' papers had to be graded and it was my job to do it. The thought of returning home on Wednesday to my old life – alone, without the possibility of him made me shudder.

I'm still here. I'll always be here with you, I heard him say. I closed my eyes against the ache in my heart.

I wish, I answered, before realizing what I had done. My eyes flew open to find a faint image of him staring back at me from in front of the mirror.

"Oh My God," I gasped. "Oh My God, I'm going crazy." The thought terrified and comforted me in the same dark place where my grief was trying to pull me down. I backed out of the bathroom as if I'd just seen a ghost.

You can't lose your mind over this, Cara. Get a hold of yourself. He's not coming back. How many times do you need to hear it? You can't just wish him back.

Yet, some corner of my heart felt sure that that was exactly what I had just done. I remember him saying, *when you're ready, come find me.* But that doesn't apply now, I reminded myself sternly. That doesn't apply to anything anymore.

I couldn't stop myself from going to the beach and dragging my chair right up to the surf just so I could be near him somehow. I pretended to grade papers under the shade of my wide-brimmed hat while watching the water ebb and flow out of the corner of my eye. I stared as the waves came together, then broke apart, moving farther and farther up the shore until all I could see was how each rush of water dissapeared into the sand as if lost forever only to reappear, asserting its existence as an endless, unbreakable force. And as I watched, I knew - Adam is still alive.

Whether trapped in some subatomic state or not, somewhere Adam was alive and I couldn't give up on him, no matter how impossible things seemed, until he wasn't.

I finished grading the rest of my papers with a small flicker of hope burning in the place my ache used to be. It was too fragile to hold much optimism, but I knew it was strong enough to survive whatever the future brought us.

I went to bed lonely that night, but calm enough to risk turning the TV on the next day. But instead of a restful sleep, I found myself tossing and turning until I felt a faint pressure on my forehead. My eyes flew open in surprise and there he was, hanging above me like a cloud. I sat up in the bed, about to scream when I heard the sound of Adam's voice in my head.

"I like this place. It took me a while to find you, but I like it."

"Adam? My God! You're here! How . . . how did you get here?" I managed to stammer. Staring at Adam's face, I saw that his lips were moving, but there was no sound coming from them. His body was there, but not, more shadow than substance in the early morning light. He was the essence of the man I loved without the man himself.

"That's exactly right. See! You understand so much without me even having to tell you."

"Adam, what's happening? If you're not here, where are you?"

His smile was gentle as the wisps of his fingers traced the curve of my cheek.

"You're even more beautiful in the morning. I knew you would be."

It hadn't occurred to me to be frightened until that moment. If Adam was avoiding my questions, the situation must have been really bad, but before I had the chance to ask him again, he answered.

"You know there was an accident. I came to you as soon as I could, but you were so sad. It seemed like me trying to comfort you only made things worse. I'm sorry, Cara. I never wanted to hurt you."

I'd cried so much over the last few days, that I didn't think I could cry anymore, but the tears came down so easily. "That was you? I thought…I told myself that I was just imagining you."

"I wanted to be here. To be with you…," his voice trailed off as he moved closer.

"But you're not here." As I reached for him, his strong, beautiful hands disintegrated between my fingers like smoke from a dying flame. Holding back tears, I asked, "Are you . . . dead?"

"No, baby. No. I'm just…separated from my body. My consciousness is here, like you said, but without my body, I'm free to travel anywhere and I can see us, Cara. In time, outside of time, and it's beautiful. I know why I love you; why I've always loved you."

"I don't understand. What do you mean? What do you see?"

"Einstein was right, Cara. At light speed, time ceases to exist. Everything is happening at once and I see us, Cara—us as we truly are, souls seeking each other throughout the expression of time. So many lifetimes we've tried to reach each other. Even if only for a moment, I've always loved you and you've always loved me."

The truth of his words clinched my heart and spilled my tears. I felt that ache in my chest again - and understood it for the first time for what it truly was, the struggle to breathe against the weight of ages of longing.

Suddenly I feel the wisps of his arms around me from behind. But, though the gesture was meant to comfort, there was no warmth, no weight to his embrace.

"I don't want a moment. I want you back. I want you back here with me!"

His feather-light head rested at the back of my neck.

"I don't know how," he whispered.

"What does that mean?"

"We don't have the technology to re-assemble my body. It's too much information. Trillions and trillions of atoms. We don't have the capacity to recreate all the connections and sequences that make up the human body. It doesn't exist, not yet."

I heard him. I understood the practical aspects of what he was saying; yet instead of despair I felt angry, defiant. *He came back to me!* Despite how impossible that was, he'd come back to me. I was only beginning to get used to the way this love made me feel and I wasn't ready to lose it. I refused to lose him again. With a sense of determination that I could barely comprehend, I turned around in the bed to face him.

"I don't accept that."

"Cara, it's true. I wouldn't lie to you. I don't want it to be true, but it is."

"No, it's not. I refuse to believe that. If what you say is true about us, I know I've never let you go willingly. I *know* that and I don't plan to start now. There has to be a way."

Adam smiled then. "No, you have never let me go willingly."

"How did you find me?"

"It's . . hard to describe. I just *felt* you, stronger than anything else. I followed your vibration until I found you. I thought of you and somehow I came here."

"Does everything have a vibration?"

"Yes. Everyone has a specific vibration that is unique to them. I can feel it clearly."

"Can you find yours?"

"Yes, but it's faint because I think consciousness is the core of that vibration. It's what makes each being unique. But, Cara, even if I return to Accra, I can't complete the teleportation sequence and just make myself a physical being again. I tried in the lab. It didn't work."

"Then how come I can see you? How are you doing it now?"

Adam was silent for a moment. "I don't know," he said finally.

"What are you thinking about? What makes you take form?"

"The desire to touch you. I *want* you to see me. I want to be with you, but Cara, I don't think it's enough."

"You don't know that."

"I don't even know how this works. Am I attracting particles or somehow creating matter with my thoughts?"

"Does it matter?"

"Cara, pulling together a few wisps of air and re-assembling an entire human body aren't the same thing—at all."

"How do you know? You're the first person ever to try it."

"Cara, there is no scientific basis for this. I . . . there's no way to know how this *could* even work."

Since I could hear him in my head, there was nothing to stop me from moving around the room as I prepared to pack my things.

"We don't know anything Adam, but if I summoned you here, maybe I can help summon you back. I'm not giving up—not if there's a chance."

By the time we finished debating, I was dressed and halfway through brushing my teeth. My plan was to check the flights to Accra on the way to the airport. With any luck, I could get a direct flight and be there by the end of the day.

"All right," Adam conceded. "I'll try to reach Dr. Nkrumah and explain to him that you're coming. This is going to be interesting."

While he was talking, I tried to rinse out my mouth as elegantly and quickly as I could.

"You did a good job. That was the most elegant teeth-rinsing I've ever seen."

I narrowed my eyes. "Can you read my thoughts?"

"Mostly, yes. But, it's more like I hear your thoughts as part of a collective consciousness, like a constant hum surrounding my own vibration. I can choose to focus on one or just become a part of the larger vibration."

"Wow," I said, amazed at everything he had access to in his current state of being.

"I know. So if this doesn't work out, my plan is to follow you around like a ghost and read your mind for the rest of your life."

He was putting on a brave face, but I could feel the fear behind his words as they rippled through my brain.

Looking at his transparent form reflected in the mirror, I tried to imagine life without ever feeling the warmth of his embrace again. The thought felt like accepting death and I shut it down before the sadness of it overwhelmed me.

"Do you remember what you promised me?" I said to his reflection.

"I do," Adam replied as he stepped forward.

"Good," I said, turning to face him. "Because haunting me is not a part of that promise, and I plan to hold you to it."

Adam let out a quick laugh, but there was no joy in it. Inside, I knew he was trying to hold on to a very thin line of hope. I knew because on the other end of that line was me.

Suddenly, his head popped up. "Hey, there is one piece of good news that almost got lost in all this."

"What's that?" I asked skeptically.

"We did what we set out to do. Jo made it. Safe and sound."

I didn't watch the news on the drive to the airport, but it didn't matter much because, by the time I got to the airport, *I* was already news, at least with the IST security team, which met me at the airport and shuttled me onto a private jet.

Once Adam made his "presence" known to the TAP team, they made arrangements to have me flown to Accra immediately. Coverage of the accident and the missing Dr. Adam Coleman was all over the news, but because of the unscientific nature of what we planned to try, no details were released. Instead, Dr. Bain explained to the press that they were gearing up for a "highly experimental technique" that would hopefully bring Dr. Coleman out of suspended animation.

I guess if you thought about it from a scientist's perspective, the idea was embarrassingly imprecise. Since Adam seemed only to be able to take physical form with me, the hope was that if he returned his consciousness with his body, somehow he would be able to use me as a beacon to take full physical form again.

On the plane ride over, in between being asked a million questions about who I was and how I knew Adam, they explained to me that since human tissue degrades overtime at varying rates, they weren't sure how teleportation would affect the re-assembly of his cells over an extended period of time. In short, we needed to act quickly before deterioration of his cell particles complicated what was already a nearly impossible problem to solve.

I arrived at the base in Accra just after 8 PM, and while I was sure no one that I met had slept much since the accident, they were all incredibly alert and desperate to try anything that would save their colleague's life. Walking into the control room, I was immediately greeted by Dr. Bain and Dr. Nkrumah, who for lack of a better expression looked like they'd just seen a ghost.

"Adam has been talking to us . . . . . .telepathically," Dr. Nkrumah began, then shook his head. "I can't believe I just said that out loud," he muttered before continuing. "He's been explaining to us the separation of his conscious energy from the physical elements that make up his body. Obviously, we were completely unprepared for anything like this."

"I'm sure," I said reassuringly. "Have you seen him?"

"No. Apparently, he's still only able to take physical form with you."

Just then, Dr. Bain stepped forward. "As much as I hate to say this, I want to make sure that you understand that there is very little chance that this will work. We can't aid in the completion of his teleportation at all. Our systems were only able to track about 50% of the particles that were dispersed during the accident. If there is more data, we simply don't have the capacity to catalog or synthesize it. What I'm saying is, are you sure you want to try this? It could kill him. At least for now, in suspended animation, he's alive."

"What did Adam tell you?

Dr. Bain crossed her arms and smiled sadly, "He's telling me now that nothing I say will dissuade either of you."

I couldn't help but smile back. "Then you should listen to him. I'm ready to start whenever you are."

"How do you see this working?" Dr. Nkrumah continued. "We have no protocol for this."

"I want to be as close to him as possible."

"Right this way, then."

※

The chamber where Adam would be 're-animated' was cold and sterile with metal that was polished to a sheen on the outside, yet almost translucent once you stepped inside. I sat on the outside of the chamber in what they called a sterile suit. Looking around me, I'd never been so far from everything I'd ever done or understood in my life. There were monitors and gadgets I'd never even heard of before, all calculating things I couldn't begin to fathom. Yet even in the midst of this, I felt close to him. This was part of his world, and by extension and necessity, it had now become a part of mine.

I closed my eyes and waited until I could feel his lips on mine, even through the suit. Through the communication link in my helmet, I could hear the collective gasps as he appeared before me, but I ignored every other sound but that of his voice.

"I wish I had touched you more. I'm sorry for that. I thought I had more time."

"We do have time. We will always have time."

I could see the tears streaking down his cloud-like face, but I couldn't reach them, even as I felt the wisps of his fingers try to wipe mine away.

"Thank you for giving me the best day of my life, Cara Morgan. It was worth it, coming all this way, just to meet you."

"And thank you, for every single day I get to spend with you after today."

"Whatever happens, I love you, Cara, and I will find you again, in this life or the next," he whispered.

"Whatever happens, I love you, too, and I promise to do the same, but first, come back to me."

Standing before him, I could feel the tenuous line of hope between us, as fragile as the ether of his form, but I refused to give into the hopelessness that pressed in around us on all sides. I needed him to do the same.

"Yes, ma'am. I'll do my best," he said finally. His voice in my head was deep and strong.

I thought I felt the slightest squeeze of my hand through my gloves, but I was too afraid to look away from his face to check. Then, before I could say another word, he was gone.

From the control room, I could hear them begin the countdown. In front of me, the chamber door slid closed, with pieces of him locked away somewhere inside. I placed my hands on the outside of the door, closed my eyes and tried to think of us.

Then I began to talk.

I told him about every single dream of him I'd had since the day we met, how many children I wanted, and how his touch made me understand why I was made a woman. I told him how I'd waited all my life to love someone the way I loved him and how grateful I was for the chance. And I told him about my plans to apply for a professorship at the University of Ghana in Accra, although we would eventually need to move back to my house in DC. I listed all my favorite songs and explained what they meant to me. I told him how I'd never smoked a cigarette, but always wanted to. I told him how much I couldn't wait to go dancing with him. I told him how I hated cats and how he'd better not have one.

I talked and I talked and I talked, through the countdown and the terrifying silence in the control room. I talked through the door that did not open and the fear that gripped me when the silence stretched long past hope. Until the door finally slid open and I fell into two strong arms.

With a euphoric mix of disbelief and pure joy, I looked up to find his beautiful, exhausted face smiling down at me. I wasted about 2 seconds in shock before I threw my arms around him and held him tight enough to never let him go.

"You're going to have to tell me all that stuff about cats and dogs again because I could barely make out a thing you were saying through all this metal," he teased.

No words would come, so I nodded instead as cheers from the control room rang in my ears.

Adam lifted my helmet off and kissed me softly on my lips, my hair, and my cheeks until finally he stopped at the curve of my ear.

"Actually, now that I think about it, you can probably tell me all that stuff later. I just remembered: I have a promise to keep."

※

It took another 6 hours for Adam to get the chance to keep his promise, but it was worth every second of the wait. As soon as we stepped out of the teleportation chamber doors we were swarmed by every scientist, administrator and custodian in the entire TAP facility.

I couldn't blame them. The last three days had been most of their worst nightmares and I could see the relief streaming down their faces as they celebrated the miracle of Adam's return. Someone even had the foresight to bring him a towel to cover himself once we were through the chamber doors because his suit and clothes didn't make it back with him.

Though his exhaustion was clear, Adam was gracious in expressing his gratitude for all their support and sharing their enthusiasm. Not sure what my role should be among this reunion of colleagues, at first I tried to give him some space, but Adam would not let go of my hand. Holding a towel around his waist with one hand and mine in the other he made his way through the crowd to Dr. Bain who stood at the back of the crowd with a small, satisfied expression on her face. When we finally reached her, the woman who expressed so little optimism for our "unscientific intervention", surprised me by embracing us both.

"It's good to see you, Adam."

"It's good to be seen," he joked back while squeezing my hand.

"I know you two want to be alone and I hate to insist, but we're going to need to run some tests right away. This is an unprecedented event, one we're not likely to see or attempt again anytime soon. But what you been through Adam, as a scientist, I know you can respect the need for answers here."

"I do understand," Adam replied. "Don't worry. Whatever you need let's just get it over with. I want to make sure that I'm alright before we move forward."

Adam turned to me then, as if wanting my approval before they proceeded. The gesture took me aback for a moment before I realized that it shouldn't have. We were in this together.

"Absolutely," I agreed. "We need to make sure you're okay."

And I meant it. I just didn't know that it would take five hours for all the testing to be done. As soon as Adam pulled on some pants it began. Hearing and vision tests, x-rays, two psychological evaluations, bone density and CAT scans, an MRI, body composition scans and stress tests. In addition, Adam had his blood taken every hour on the hour. They practically flooded him with water just to get a urine sample. And in between all this, Adam was swabbed, scraped and probed relentlessly. His patience with all of it was unfailing until the physician in charge of his assessment, Dr. Reid, asked him for sperm sample.

Throughout most of Adam's testing I was either at his side or very nearby. I'd just returned with a glass of orange juice to counteract all the bloodletting when Dr. Reid asked his question. In the short time that I'd known Adam, I never seen him even remotely annoyed until that moment. His eyes flashed to Dr. Reid who was directly in front of him, then to me.

"No," he said flatly. "I'm going to need that for something else….soon I hope."

Dr. Reid looked up from his paperwork.

"If you think you can't…" Dr. Reid began before catching sight of me as I slid into the chair beside Adam and handed him the cup of orange juice.

"Oh…Oh!" He said. "Well…um. I don't mean to pry, but do you think you will be using a condom?"

If I could've turned beet red, I would have, but Adam didn't miss a beat.

"I hadn't planned on getting her pregnant our first-time together. I'd like us to spend a little more time together, you know, get married before we start a family."

"Yes, of course. I mean - I know this is highly irregular. I was just suggesting that if you used a condom, you could store it, so that afterwards we could…"

I'm not sure what my expression looked like, but Adam's must've been something to behold because Dr. Bain practically leapt from her chair in the corner of the room to interrupt.

"Dr. Reid, I think that'll be all for now. The press is getting antsy. The rest of us have tried to appease them, but they really need to hear from Adam. It's time."

Adam gave Dr. Reid an icy stare before he rose from the table with my hand in his. I followed him out, fully expecting to be ushered to some back area while he took the stage, but as we approached the press area, he didn't let go.

"Adam." I said pulling back. "It's you they want to hear from. I'll just wait for you here."

Though I was used to speaking in front of a crowd, I wasn't sure if I was up for facing a room full of reporters. Adam turned and looked at me for a long time. His face was even more drawn than when I'd seen him right after his teleportation, but his eyes shown with that same light they held our first night together.

"This is our story, Cara," he said finally. "Yours and mine to tell for the rest of our lives. Just 30 minutes and we'll be out of there. I promise."

We walked onto the stage to thunderous applause and blinding lights. It was unlike anything I'd ever experienced before and, by the look on Adam's face, I could tell he felt the same. Up until that moment, I'd been thinking of this journey as just ours, but looking out at the cameras and all the eager faces waiting to hear from us, I realized just how much energy, faith and hope people all around the world had poured into bringing Adam back to me. Adam pulled out my seat as we sat down to face the world together.

"Good evening and thank you all for your prayers and your patience. I'm grateful to have made it back in one piece and be here with you tonight. For those of you who don't know me, I'm Dr. Adam Coleman and this woman beside me is Dr. Cara Morgan. She is the reason I'm sitting here before you. Her courage and her faith gave me the strength to find my way back home."

I looked at Adam stunned; he looked right back at me and smiled. When he took my hand again, I felt the energy between us, coursing stronger than it had ever felt. Together, we answered questions and expressed our gratitude. We talked and shared as much as we could until 29 minutes in, Adam announced that we were both exhausted and needed to rest. After one last round of thank yous, Adam escorted me out of the pressroom.

We walked down a pathway I hadn't seen before, and though the halls were filled with well wishers and curious stares, no one got in our way.

All of the fatigue and anxiety of the day melted away as he closed the door to his living quarters behind us and shut out the world. Our love-making was languid, yet passionate and unlike anything I had ever experienced before. Every touch, though new, felt familiar, comforting and exactly right, as if we'd known each other's bodies completely, right from the start. And afterwards, as we lay intertwined with our bodies bathed in the first light of a new day, I couldn't think of a better way to start the rest of our lives together.

Other books by
CERECE RENNIE MURPHY

SCIENCE FICTION

Order of the Seers (Book I)
Order of the Seers: The Red Order (Book II)
Order of the Seers: The Last Seer (Book III)

EARLY READER CHAPTER BOOKS
WWW.THEELLISSERIES.COM

Ellis and The Magic Mirror
Ellis and The Hidden Cave (Coming 2016)

Learn more and read excerpts from each of these titles at
WWW.CERECERENNIEMURPHY.COM

About
CERECE RENNIE MURPHY

Cerece Rennie Murphy fell in love with writing and science fiction at an early age. It's a love affair that has grown ever since.

In addition to working on the release of the 2nd book in the Ellis and The Magic Mirror children's book series with her son, Mrs. Murphy is developing a 2-part science fiction thriller set in outer space. Mrs. Murphy lives and writes in her hometown of Washington, DC with her husband, two children and the family dog, Yoda. To learn more about the author and her upcoming projects, please visit her website at

WWW.CERECERENNIEMURPHY.COM